THORN'S REDEMPTION

FATED LIVES SERIES

KELLY MOORE

Edited by
KERRY GENOVA

Cover Designer
DARK WATER COVERS

TITLE

THORN'S
REDEMPTION

KELLY MOORE

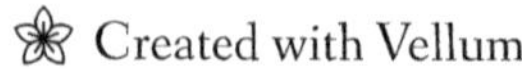
Created with Vellum

THORN BECKHAM

CHAPTER 1

MY RESISTANCE

"Would you try to keep up, Son." My dad's voice booms from in front of me.

"I've already told you I don't want to join the Navy, so why are you making me do this?"

He halts his movement, turning around to cast a staunch glare in my direction. "You can't make a living tinkering around with cars all day. You need structure and discipline."

"Has it ever occurred to you that's all I've ever had, except that we've moved so many times I've lost count."

"You're military born and bred." He waves a stern finger at me. "All Beckham men for the last three generations have served this country."

"I know. I've heard it a hundred times before, but

it doesn't change the fact that it's not what I want for my life."

An infinitesimal twitch in his bottom lip tells me he's trying to rein in his anger. I stand two inches taller than him and outweigh him by fifty pounds, but being the true soldier he is, he's never let my size intimidate him. He blows out a breath for control, then places a firm grip on my shoulder. "Thorn, I know this life hasn't been easy on you growing up."

"That's putting it mildly." His look scolds me for interrupting him.

"It's different when you're an adult. There is no other job like it."

"Why can't you understand it's not the life I want? I love working on cars, and I don't want to move again. I like Florida where it's hot and sunny every day. I like living in the Panhandle. It has the bluest water I've ever laid eyes on."

He takes a step back and scratches his chin. "This is about Eden, isn't it?"

"No...yes. She doesn't want to be a military wife."

"Wife?" His hands drop to his sides.

"Yes. I asked her to marry me."

"You're too young to get married. You haven't had time to figure out what you want yet."

"Dad, I'm twenty-one. Eden and I've been dating since we were sixteen."

"Out of the five years you've been dating, how much have you actually seen the girl?"

"That's because we move every time we turn around. We talk all the time. I'm done moving from place to place. I want to settle down and start my own life with Eden."

He spins in a circle on his heels. Captain Bruce Beckham is not a man easily flustered. He runs a tight ship, but when it comes to his only son, the ship has sunk. We've never seen eye-to-eye. I have great respect for what he does, but he's never let me make my own choices. My mother, Carole, caterers to him and loves being a Navy wife.

"Let's finish this conversation later. I've got a limited window of time to take you up in the helicopter."

"Fine, I'll do this and go to the shooting range if you agree that if I decide it's not for me, you'll drop it."

He clenches his jaw but finally gives in. "Deal. Now come on before they cancel my plans."

I have to pick up the pace to keep up with him. Whiting Field has one of the best airstrips in the military. Everything from the hangars, airplanes, helicopters, and runway are well maintained.

We make it to the airfield, and he grabs a clipboard off the hangar wall and fills out the paperwork. He steps inside the glass door to the small office, coming back out with a helmet and headphones.

"Put these on once we get inside."

He leads me over to a burnt red-colored helicopter. I climb in one of the two bucket seats and immediately strap into it. There are windows all around. Digital displays, a dashboard with indicators, a compass, knob controls, and two joysticks to fly the helicopter.

"Don't touch anything until I tell you to." My dad barks orders.

I tug on my helmet and place the headset over my ears. I dig my Ray-Bans out and finagle them in place.

Dad does the same and checks all the equipment. He talks to someone through his earphones and mouthpiece, getting clearance for us to take off. There's an escalating whine as the engine starts up. The next noise is the choppy sound of the blades as they start spinning, cutting through the air. I grab onto the netting, holding on as the chopper lifts off the ground. The seat belt jolts against my shoulder as he raises the joystick for us to go higher.

As we rise further into the air, the chopper tilts and sways. I keep expecting to feel that dropping sensation in my gut, but I don't. Instead, I feel the surge of adrenaline pumping through me. It's an instant love for something I thought I'd hate. We continue to go higher and higher until we level out. The scenery is beautiful. Totally different looking down on the blue waters of the Gulf.

"Do you want to fly it?" My father's gaze cuts to me.

I nod.

"Gently take ahold of the joystick. Don't make any sudden movements with it."

I place my left hand on it, and the slightest movement makes the chopper wobble, but I get a feel for it quickly. "This is awesome!" I yell so he can hear me over the sound of the whirling blades.

"I had a feeling you'd like it!" he says back and does something he rarely does with me...smiles.

He's right. I've always loved cars, trucks, basically anything with an engine. I don't know why I thought this would be any different. I can see why he likes this part so much. It doesn't mean I'd have to join the military to fly.

"Take us lower," his voice is loud.

I push the joystick to take us down, closer to the water. The lush blue of the water is gorgeous. It's smooth and clear.

"Dolphins!" He points.

There's an entire school of them playing on top of the water. He takes control of the stick and hugs the water so close I'd swear I could hang my foot out and drag it in the warmth of the Gulf. Flying in a helicopter is totally different than a plane. It maneuvers easily, and I like the feeling of control and the fact that you can get close to the land.

"Imagine flying this baby with your men in the back, getting ready to jump onto the land. The pilot has to have mad skills to maintain steadiness of this beast. Your men are counting on you to hold firm. They put their lives on the line to keep the country safe. There's no better job. I'm proud of every one of the men and women who dedicate their lives to this to keeping us out of harm's way."

I'm seeing a vastly different side of him than I'm used to. He takes pride in his job and being a leader. I understand why he'd want that for me. I've always thought of him as having a cold demeanor, I'm thinking now, it's something else. Strength and focus come to mind.

He lets me take the bird back to the Navy base, taking the controls back right before we land. I pull my gear off and unbuckle. I hop out and wait for him to come back out of the office. When he walks up to me, he puts his arm around my shoulder. "Nice job. You'd make a great pilot, Son."

"Thanks for letting me fly. It was really cool."

"You're welcome."

"Do you want to head over to the shooting range?"

He looks at his watch. "I'd like to, but I'm afraid I have a meeting to go to. Don't let that keep you from going. You have your ID. You shouldn't have any problems getting in without me."

"Do you think I could try your AR-15?" I've been wanting to shoot it.

"Absolutely, get it out of the gun safe. Just make sure you clean it when you're done."

We part ways, and I get in my Chevy to head home. I decide to call Eden on the way to tell her all about flying the helicopter.

"Hey, babe."

"Hey, Thorn."

"You'll never believe what I did today."

"Um...fixed a motorcycle," she says sarcastically, knowing that I've been working on one.

"I flew a helicopter with my dad."

"Is he still trying to convince you to follow in his footsteps?"

"Every day." I chuckle. "I fell in love with it."

"You know you don't have to be in the service to fly?"

"Would it be so bad if I changed my mind? My dad telling me about soldiers jumping out and needing a good pilot inspired me." Her momentary silence on the other end tells me it would be an issue.

"We've talked about this. I don't want to be a soldier's wife. I'd always be worried about you, and I don't ever want to leave my hometown."

"I know, you're right. It's not what I want either." At least it was never a consideration until today. "I love you."

"Love you, too."

"How about I come see you next week. I can take a few days off at the shop and catch a quick flight to Asheville."

"I'd love that."

We met in high school when my dad had a short stint at the US Navy Department in Asheville, North Carolina. Eden was the first person I met. She's the sweetest southern girl with blonde hair and big blue eyes. I don't know how I got so lucky. All the boys in school were in love with her, but she only had eyes for me. She's a dental hygienist and loves her work. I only went to school there a year before we moved again. I wanted to move back there after I graduated, but Mom had just been diagnosed with multiple sclerosis and wasn't doing well. Dad was traveling at the time to different military bases, instructing classes. She needed someone to stick around. I enrolled in the technical school and studied how to be a mechanic. Mom's in remission, so Eden and I've been talking about getting married. I can scope out some job opportunities when I go visit her.

"I gotta go. Call me tonight before you go to bed. I'll buy my ticket between now and then and let you know the specifics."

"Bye, Thorn. Love you."

CHAPTER 2

THE SHOOTING RANGE

The indoor military shooting range is not the typical range you'd see out around town. It doesn't have racks of guns on the walls behind glass displays, or items for sale like pepper spray, mace, whistles, holsters, or cleaning kits. No, this is badge-in only. You can bring your own weapon that has to be inspected or have one issued to you.

I carry in the duffel bag with my father's AR-15 and a box of ammunition, along with two magazines. I've been here a few times with my dad, but never by myself. I'm thinking his sudden meeting is some type of trap that will lure me into wanting to sign up.

I flash my ID without any problems and grab protective earmuffs and eye gear that are tossed on the counter while the instructor inspects my weapon.

Before I head into the range, I take a silhouette target and tuck it under my arm.

I put on my headphones and eyewear then I'm buzzed into the range area that has foam walls to absorb the sound. Finding an empty numbered lane behind bulletproof glass partitions, I set my bag down then take out the AR-15. I test the weight of the weapon in my hand by moving it up and down and placing the butt of it against my shoulder. I grip the rough grid of plastic on the weapon to get a feel for it. Once I'm comfortable, I take out the ammo and load the magazines. I place my target on the clip and push the button that moves it downrange, stopping it seventy-five yards out.

Shifting my feet from side to side, I find the right balance as I grip the rifle. Steadying my breath to find a calm place to take a shot, I brush my finger against the trigger, fully committed to pulling it, feeling the slight resistance. As I aim, squeezing the trigger, sending several rounds downrange, massacring my target. My eyes instinctively blink at the sound, but I hold strong in my focus. I love the concussive thunder I feel in my chest every time a bullet is released. I get a prick of adrenaline firing such a powerful weapon. It's not the same as holding a gun in your hand. Its power becomes a part of you.

I lower my weapon and push the button, bringing the target toward me. I can hear the sounds of other weapons being fired even though my ears are covered.

A tap on my shoulder has me turning around and raising my left earmuff to hear the range instructor say in a deep, baritone voice, "That's some damn good shooting, son."

"Thanks."

"Aren't you Captain Bruce Beckham's son?"

He knows good and well who I am. He's seen me many times in here with my father. "You already know who I am." I chuckle.

"You caught me. Your father wanted me to speak with you and test your gun-handling abilities." He points to the target. "Best I've seen in a young guy in a long time."

"Let me guess. He wants you to convince me to join the Navy." I glance over my shoulder at him.

"I'm not going to lie to you, son, he does, but after what I just saw, the military needs men like you. With that aim, you could become a Navy SEAL."

Now that would interest me, but I don't dare let on. "I have other things in mind for my life. I know what my dad wants, but it's not for me."

"Well, if you change your mind, I'd gladly send

in a recommendation for you."

"I won't, but thanks."

"Do you mind if I stay here and watch?"

"Suit yourself." I replace my target and resume shooting. The more I handle the rifle, the easier it gets, and the easier it gets, the more I hear his words "you could become a SEAL." I like the thought, but Eden has made it very clear it's not what she wants.

When I finally run out of ammo, I load the rifle in the duffel bag and head out to the main part of the building where I can clean my weapon. I return the headphones and safety glasses into a bin before I spend the next hour carefully cleaning my dad's rifle.

I look up and see my dad talking to the instructor. I can hear him now in my head, asking how I did. They chat back and forth for a few minutes, then shake hands.

I'm putting the last piece of the rifle back together when he ends up by my side. "The range instructor tells me you're good. Of course, I already knew that, but someone else needed to evaluate your skills."

"Eden is never going to go for it." I stuff the rifle in the duffel.

"This isn't about Eden. It's about what you want to do with your life."

"Eden is part of that. She should have a say in it too."

"Look, Son, I know you think you love this girl, but your career should be first."

I let out a sigh. "I'll talk to Eden this weekend face-to-face. If she doesn't feel she can handle being a military wife, then there is nothing else to talk about."

His jaw flexes a few times. "You have too much talent to waste."

"I'm sorry it's not what you want for my life, but it's my decision." I zip up the bag and throw the strap over my shoulder. "We'll talk about it when I get back from Asheville."

* * *

"Absolutely not!" Eden is adamant.

"You don't have to leave here. We've been doing the long-distance relationship and making it work."

"That's not how I want my marriage to be. If you join, you know you'll have no control over where they send you."

People in the restaurant are starting to stare at us. I reach over and hold her hand. "What if it's something I want to do? Generations of my family have served." I talk softly. "Are you really telling me if I join we're over?"

She drags her hand out of mine and relaxes back. "No," she finally says with a huff.

I get up from my side of the booth and join her, wrapping my arm around her shoulder. "We can make this work, baby."

"I need to know why you've changed your mind?" Her bottom lip is in a full-out pout.

"Honestly, when my dad took me up in the helicopter, something in me changed. I loved it, and shooting his rifle reinforced that feeling. I loved the feel of chopper in my hands as much as the rifle. It fueled something in me I didn't know existed. If you felt that way about something, I'd never keep you from it."

"I know I'm being selfish, but I can't do it. My life is here."

I drop my arm in my lap. "Okay, then I won't do it. We'll get married, and I'll move here and open up a shop."

"Seriously?" She squeals and drapes her arms around me.

"You're more important to me." I love her, but I can't help but feel I just gave up a part of me that was meant to do something great.

CHAPTER 3

MY GREATEST LOSS

"Yes, Mom. Eden and I've settled in nicely in our new home." I listen on the phone as she rattles off numerous questions. I think she still misses me even though Eden and I married a year ago, and I moved to North Carolina. We bought a house last month, and Eden's been slowly buying furniture to fill it up. I started working for the Chevy dealer in the service department. It's not the greatest job, but I'm saving up to buy my own garage.

"Your father says he has time off next week and we'll come for a visit." She sounds so excited.

"We'd love that." I'd like to see my mom, but my relationship with my dad has been strained since I told him I was marrying Eden, and not joining the military. I hate that he's disappointed in me. It's bad enough that I'm disappointed in myself. I've yet to shake the feeling that I was meant to follow in his footsteps. He's cordial to my wife, but his eyes give him away. He blames her for my decision and keeps an arm's distance relationship with her. My mom, on the other hand, adores her.

"I'll let you know the details before we make our way there. Give Eden my love."

"I will, Mom."

I grab leftovers from the fridge and head to work. We've got our routine down pretty well. Eden leaves for work at seven in the morning and is home by four. I have a later shift, going in at ten and off at six. We enjoy spending our evenings together snuggled up on the couch. I have a hot little wife who loves me, what more could I ask for?

Several cars and two trucks are in the holding area when I get to work. The bays are already filled up with other mechanics working on repairs. I change out of my clothes and into my work uniform. Grabbing the clipboard with the next customer's name on it, I get their vehicle and start my day.

An hour later, I'm buried underneath a lifted truck when someone tugs on my foot. "Hey, you have an urgent phone call."

I push myself out from underneath to see my

boss's face. "Are you sure I can't call whoever it is back?" I take the rag from my back pocket and wipe the grease from my hands. I don't bring my cell phone into the shop, so it's rare that I get a call.

"It's your mom. She sounds upset."

I jump off the floor and run into the small office area and pick up the line that's blinking red. "Mom, you okay?"

"It's your father," she cries.

"What's wrong with dad?"

"He was complaining this morning that he wasn't feeling well, but he sucked it up and went to work anyway," she sniffs.

"What happened?"

"He collapsed. His men performed CPR." Her words barely come out through her sobs.

"Where is he?" My voice cracks.

"He was taken to the local hospital. He's on life support. They told me to call you to tell you to get here quickly."

"I'll get the next flight out and get there as soon as I can." I hang up with her and call Eden to let her know what happened. She'll work on getting me a flight so I can shower and change clothes. As soon as I'm done, I go straight to the airport. She was able to get a quick flight purchased.

* * *

I hail a cab and rush straight to the hospital, calling my mom on the way.

"Please tell me you've made it here?" She's still crying.

"I'm in a cab headed your direction. What room is he in?"

"He's in the intensive care unit room 202."

"Any changes?"

"The doctor said he had a massive heart attack."

I'm in shock because he's always been so healthy and in good shape. "Can you drive faster?" I cover the phone and yell at the cab driver, who picks up the speed. "I'll be there in ten minutes, Mom." I hang up and make a quick call to Eden to let her know I've landed.

The cab driver pulls up to the main entrance of the hospital, and I rush inside, stopping only to wait for the elevator. I'm buzzed in on the second floor once I've told them who I'm here to see. A young nurse escorts me to his room where he's hooked up to all types of machines. Mom is standing by his side holding his hand. Her tears flow harder when she sees me.

"Thorn," she cries, rushing over to hug me.

I kiss the top of her head. “It’s okay, Mom.”

“The doctor said he’s in grave condition.”

She walks me over to his bed. His eyes are closed, and his brows are drawn downward. His skin looks gray and clammy. I bend down and get close to his ear. “Dad, can you hear me? It’s Thorn, I’m here.”

His head moves slightly, and his eyes peek open. “Son,” he says barely over a whisper.

I place my hand on his chest. “Are you in any pain?”

He doesn’t answer the question. “I’m sorry,” he says.

“You’ve nothing to be sorry for, Dad.”

“I’m sorry I messed things up for you.”

“You didn’t mess anything up. What are you talking about?”

“Moving you all over the country, forcing you to be part of a life that you walked away from.”

“I don’t regret any of it. I’ve had a good life.”

He shakes his head. “I was too hard on you.”

“No you weren’t. You’ve taught me so much and only wanted the best for me. I love you for that. I’m sorry that I disappointed you.” My warm tears start to roll down my face. I swipe them away on my shoulder.

“I’m proud of you for standing up for yourself.”

He swallows hard. "I love you, boy." He closes his eyes, and the alarms go off, sending in a barrage of nurses, doctors, and a code cart.

I take mom out of the room, and we watch in slow motion, as it all goes down. Mom loses it when the doctor calls time of death.

Everything after that day was a whirlwind between the military funeral, helping Mom pack up and leave the base, moving her to North Carolina with us, and dealing with the loss of my father. It affected me more than I ever imagined. I wanted to fill his shoes, and the only way I could think to honor him was to follow my gut. I knew more than ever where I belonged, but signing up for the Navy would go against what my wife wanted.

CHAPTER 4

DEPLOYMENT

"Please don't do this. I'm begging you. You said so yourself that your dad reconciled with your decision before he died." Eden is pulling at my arm, trying to stop me from getting into the car to meet with a recruiter.

"I need to do this for me, not for him."

"We agreed that neither one of us wanted this life."

"I only agreed because it was what you wanted. Why can't you understand that it's what I really want to do no matter how much I've fought it?" I stop and place my hand against her cheek. "You don't have to leave here. We can make this work. I'm not asking you to follow me around the world. I'm only asking you to love me enough to let me do this."

Her tears fall, but her eyes soften. "I do love you."

I hug her to me, and she tucks her head under my chin. "That's all we need, baby."

One month later…

"Are you all packed and ready to go?" My mother is holding a box in her hand.

"I am. How are you liking your new apartment?"

"It's great. I've already made some new friends."

"Good, I'm glad to hear it."

She sits next to me on the couch. "I brought you something." She hands me a wooden box.

"This was Dad's." I recognize it. It used to sit on top of his dresser. Opening it, there are some old photographs of him and my mom shortly after they were married, his military watch, and his purple heart. "Why are you giving me these?"

"Because he'd want you to have them." She picks up one of the pictures. "I've never told you this, but I was like Eden. I didn't want this life either. I was so afraid that he'd forget all about me, but he took these pictures with me everywhere he went."

"Are you saying that's what my wife is afraid of, that I'll forget her?"

"I think that's part of it."

I drape my arm around her shoulder, pulling her in for a hug. "Thanks, Mom."

"Your dad would be so proud of you." I hear her sniffle.

"I wish I would've signed up when he was still alive to see it. I'd give anything to see him out in the crowd after boot camp."

She pats my chest. "He'll be there looking down on you, don't you worry." I kiss the top of her head as Eden walks into the room, dragging my suitcase behind her.

"It's time to go to the airport." She's had worry etched on her face for the past month.

Mom picks up her purse. "I'm going to get out of here so you don't miss your plane."

She wraps her arms around my waist. "I love you, Mom."

"Love you too, Thorn. Call me when you can."

"I will."

I take the suitcase from Eden and place the contents of the box inside, and we follow Mom out to her car. I throw my luggage in the bed of my truck and get behind the wheel as Eden climbs in the passenger's side.

"You can still change your mind." She half smiles.

I grab her hand and kiss the back of it. "I'm not changing my mind, and you've nothing to worry about. I'll always come home to you."

She's quiet on the drive to the airport. I glance over at her a few times to see tears streaming down her face. I hate that she's unhappy. I'll have to prove to her that this won't change things between us. I'll be at the mercy of the Navy, but I'll do my best to make her feel loved and not forgotten.

I pull into the departure zone and park next to the curb. I grab my bags out of the back and meet Eden on the sidewalk.

"I wish I could walk you to the gate." She wipes her tears.

"No more crying. We're going to be fine." I take her in my arms and kiss her sweet, salty lips. "I love you, baby. I'll call you the minute I can." I let go, and she doesn't release my hand until the last possible step away from her.

"I love you, Thorn."

I show my ID and make it through security

without any glitches. The gate area seating is full, so I stand by the window, watching planes roll in and out. An excitement like I've not had in a long time fills me. This is my destiny, what I was born to do.

Eight weeks of boot camp, twenty-four weeks of underwater demolition/SEAL school, and twenty-eight weeks SEAL qualification training, and I'm finally done. Only one percent of sailors who take these courses complete them. Not only did I make it, I finished with the highest rankings. I've slimmed down, and I'm a six-foot-four wall of muscle. It was the hardest thing I've ever done. Not once did I want to give up, even though at times I thought I might die.

I was hoping to get some time off before I deployed on my first assignment, but the urgency of the mission overruled me getting any leave. I've not been able to talk to Eden a lot, but when I have, we've spent hours on the phone catching up. I miss her like crazy, but I'm so focused and psyched about what I'm doing that I don't have a lot of time to think about it, unlike my wife.

Her letters come in piles at a time. I've enjoyed

reading them in the spare minutes that I can find. She sent me a picture of our wedding day, which I keep close beside me. I tuck it in my bag and board the military plane with the other men heading overseas to various bases. I plan on catching up on my sleep for the majority of the trip, so I find the most comfortable spot that I can.

That was only the beginning of my journey. I learned to pilot a chopper, and it flooded me with memories of my dad. Here I am in real life, dropping men to the ground like we talked about the one time I flew with him. I love it, but I want more. I want to be on the ground with them. We rotate different positions within the SEAL team until each of us find our niche. I'm pretty damn good at everything I try, and it isn't long before I become the team leader. I thrive at it. My trips home become few and far between.

CHAPTER 5

MY MARRIAGE STARTS TO CRUMBLE

"What do you mean your leave got postponed? You're supposed to be here tomorrow. It's our fifth anniversary." Her voice is laced with disappointment.

"I'm sorry, babe. It's only delayed a couple of days. Our mission took a little longer than expected, and I have to stay around for debriefing."

"Did you put in your request to be stationed at Camp Lejeune? You'd make a great instructor, and I could easily get a job in that area."

"I said I was considering it down the road when I've had my fill of being a SEAL."

"What about what I want? You've only been home twice this year." Now she's angry. "All I ever do is worry about you."

I can't argue with her; she's right. "I'll make it up to you. I have some extra leave time. I can stay longer this trip."

"You staying longer doesn't fix the problem. You've promised me over and over that things would get easier, and they haven't."

I beat the cell phone on my forehead. "Can we talk about it when I get home?"

* * *

Unfortunately, plans changed, and I'm just now making it back six weeks later. I decided to surprise her in case something else went wrong. I catch a cab from the airport and head straight home.

"Eden! Honey, I'm home." She's not downstairs. I lay my bags down and take the stairs two at a time. Our bedroom door is shut, and no light is on. I open it and see Eden lying in the bed asleep. I kick off my shoes and sit softly on the side of the bed, placing my hand in the middle of her back.

"Hey, baby. I'm home."

She lifts her head and opens her eyes, then rolls over. "I didn't know you were coming home. I would've picked you up." She draws the sheet up to her chin.

"It's the middle of the day. What are you doing in bed?"

"I haven't felt well." She looks down.

I crawl up in the bed next to her and hold her in my arms. "I'm here now. I'll take care of you."

Her body starts to tremble.

"What's wrong? I thought you'd be happy to see me?" I hold her tighter.

"I am." She starts to cry.

"Hey, what is it? Tell me?"

"I was pregnant."

My mind starts calculating the last time I was home. Six months ago. She's been pregnant for six months and never told me? "You lost the baby? Why didn't you tell me you were pregnant?"

"Would it have made any difference?" She pushes out of my arms.

"You think because I'm on a mission I wouldn't care that my wife was carrying my child?" Not only did she keep it from me, but now I found out our baby is gone. I run my hands over my short hair.

"It's your fault I lost the baby. I do nothing but worry about you every time you go on a mission. I don't hear from you for days on end, not knowing whether you're dead or alive. My body couldn't handle that kind of stress. I've told you for years I didn't want this life, and you selfishly did it anyway." She's out of bed, rummaging through drawers to find something to wear.

"I thought you'd eventually settle into this life."

"Settle in? How am I supposed to do that a million miles away from you?" Her face has reddened.

"You could've come with me. You chose not to. You were so determined to stay in this town. That was more important to you than being stationed to wherever I was."

"Don't talk to me about more important. Your precious SEAL team is your family. Not me!" She's screaming.

"Look. Yelling at each other isn't going to solve anything. Please sit down and talk to me so we can work this out."

"There is no we. It's always what you want. It's been that way since the day your father died. It's like a switched flipped in you, and you became someone different than the man I married."

"What are you saying? You want a divorce?" My heart sinks.

"I want us to be a team, and if you can't do that, then yes, I want out."

"What is it you want me to do? Tell me?"

"I want you to take the job that was offered to you at the base at Camp Lejeune. I want us to go to marriage counseling."

This is all happening so fast. I'm not ready to give up being a SEAL, but I'm seriously not ready to lose my wife. I stand, pacing the floor. "Okay." I finally stop in front of her, kneeling on the floor. I'll do whatever you want."

"Really?" She smiles and jumps into my arms.

"Thank you, thank you." She kisses my face.

"I'm sorry about the baby." I lean back and look into her eyes that dart away from mine. "I don't want to lose you." I pick her up and spend the rest of the day making love to my wife. As good as it feels, a part of me already starts to grieve the loss of my command.

Over the next couple of weeks, I arrange my transfer, pack up our house, and move us to base housing. My job has me at home every night, but things between the two of us remain strained. I gather it's all me because I'm hating what I'm doing and want to be back with my men.

"Don't forget, we have our first marriage counseling meeting today." Eden catches me before I make it out the door.

I glance at my watch. "What time?"

"I scheduled it for three o'clock. It's the only appointment I could get. We got worked in on a cancellation."

"Okay, I'll be there." I stress about the meeting all day at work. To have to admit to my wife that I'd rather be somewhere else is not what I want to do. Maybe the therapist can help me figure out how to not be a SEAL anymore so that my wife won't hate me.

Ten till three, I walk into the stale-looking waiting room. One disadvantage of being a doc in the military—you don't get the plush office or the income. Your patients are assigned to you.

I mindlessly flip through my phone, waiting for my wife. The office door with a metal plate with the name Dr. Lauryn Ruth opens. A tall, beautiful, leggy blonde with silky hose and heels walks out with a file in her hand.

She looks at me and smiles, sticking her hand out. "I assume you're Thorn Beckham."

I take her hand in mine, and the oddest thing happens; tingles run up my arm. I let go like she shocked me. Her expression says she felt it too. She clears her throat. "Where's your wife?"

"She should be here any minute." As if on cue, she walks through the door.

"Hey. Sorry I'm late. Traffic was terrible."

"Actually, you're right on time." Dr. Ruth introduces herself, and we walk into her office, sitting on opposite ends of the couch. She pulls up a chair and grabs a note pad.

It was the longest hour of my life. I listened as my wife complained about every decision I'd made since my father died. I think she blames him as much as she blames me. Dr. Ruth tried to redirect her a few times, but my wife had been holding it in for years and had to get it all out.

CHAPTER 6

THE TRUTH COMES OUT

"This is the fourth time we're meeting with her, and we've gotten nowhere," I whisper to Eden as we're sitting in Dr. Ruth's waiting room. Our fighting has gotten worse after every meeting.

"Maybe if you'd open up, we'd make progress." She crosses her arms over her chest.

Thank god Dr. Ruth comes out before we get into a heated argument. We take our usual positions, placing distance between the two of us on the couch.

"I want to start by saying that I've requested some one-on-one counseling with you." She speaks directly to me.

"Is that necessary?" I fidget.

"It's my professional opinion that you need to talk about the things you've done and seen as a

SEAL. You keep so much inside. I think it would help if you could share things in a safe space."

I nod. Not what I want to do.

"I want to talk about the day you came home, and your wife told you she'd lost the baby. How did that make you feel?"

"I felt bad, but I was angry she never told me about the baby in the first place." I use my hands to talk.

"Why didn't you tell him?" She turns her gaze to Eden.

"Because it wouldn't have made him come home any sooner." My wife squirms in her seat.

"If it were me, I would've thought quite the opposite." It's not a question, but a statement by Dr. Ruth.

Eden wrings her hands in her lap.

Dr. Ruth adjusts her glasses. "How far along were you when you lost the baby?"

"What difference does that make?" I defend my wife.

"Well, after the baby reaches a certain gestational age, a casket is required to bury the baby. Have you been to his gravesite?"

Eden's face turns ashen at her question.

I draw a knee up on the couch to look at her.

"Did you bury our baby and never told me that either?"

"No," she whispers.

"No what?"

"I was only eight weeks pregnant." She says it so softly, I know that I heard her wrong.

"What did you say?"

Eden's tears stream down her cheeks. I look between her and Dr. Ruth, trying to get an answer.

"You need to tell him the truth, Eden," Dr. Ruth says. "He deserves to know."

I stand. "What do I deserve to know?" My voice is loud.

"He doesn't deserve anything! He abandoned me and it's all his fault!" she cries.

"What the fuck am I missing? Tell me?" I move beside her.

"I was eight weeks pregnant when I miscarried."

"I'm still not understanding what you're telling me. So you didn't tell me right when it happened just like you didn't tell me you were pregnant."

"Thorn, have a seat, and let her get it out." Dr. Ruth is firm.

I sit and wait.

"The day before you came home, I had miscarried." Eden doesn't look at me.

"But I hadn't been home for six months..."

"I was lonely, and you were never home."

"You cheated on me?" I can't believe the words coming out of my mouth. Not once did I even look at another woman.

"It just happened. I didn't mean for it to."

"You didn't mean for some guy's dick to be inside you?" I'm up on my feet again. "Wait, oh this is good. You weren't even going to tell me it wasn't my child. You wanted me to mourn the loss of a baby that belonged to some asshole who fucked my wife while I was on a mission fighting for this country!"

"I'm sorry," she says.

"You're sorry!" I yell and slam my fist on Dr. Ruth's desk. I throw my hands in the air. "I'm done here." I swing open the door and head to my truck. Dr. Ruth is screaming my name. "Thorn!"

I wheel around to face her. "What?"

"I'm sorry. You needed to know. Her medical records came to me, and I put the pieces together. With that being said, I still want our one-on-one sessions. It's important that you be able to talk about everything that's happened."

"Yeah, well fuck that." I open the truck door.

"I can force you to come, please don't make me do that." Her fingers land on my open window.

I run my hand over my hair and pull my hat on. "Give me a few days to figure out how to deal with this mess. I'll set up an appointment next week." I turn over the ignition and squeal out of the parking lot.

I don't head home. The bar and a bourbon sound like an invitation to kill what's left of me. I drown my sorrows to the point that I start blaming myself for the affair. I'm angry as hell, but she's right. I was never there for her. How could I pin it all on her? A few more drinks in me, and I figure out how to blame her. I would've never cheated on her. And the baby! Not even mine!

The bartender throws me out and calls me a cab. He asks for my address, and I stare into space. How am I supposed to go back home? She betrayed me, and that's something you never do to anyone.

Instead of going back to the house, I sleep it off in a hotel room. I wake up with a horrible headache and ten text messages from Eden wanting to know when I'm coming home so we can talk.

It's the weekend, and I don't need to go into the office today. An office that I've come to hate. I get a ride back to the bar to pick up my truck and head home to face the inevitable. Eden is sitting at the dining room table, sipping on a cup of coffee. I let out a long sigh when I sit across from her.

"How did we get here?"

"You know my answer to that." She glares at me.

"I'm sorry that I turned into someone you didn't want me to be. I should've never convinced myself that I was anything less than a soldier at heart. For that, I'm truly sorry. I tried to be what you wanted me to be."

She gets up and sits next to me. "I was always honest with you about how I felt." She takes my hand. "We can still work this out."

I yank my hand from her. "There is nothing left between us to work out. You slept with another man and lied about the baby."

"Please, you were never here. You are now, and things are out in the open. We can keep going to see Dr. Ruth. I still love you, Thorn."

"Therein lies the problem. You killed what love I had for you the moment you admitted to cheating on me."

"I know you're angry, you don't really mean that," she cries.

"I do mean it with every fiber of my body. No amount of therapy is going to change that. I'm miserable at this job, and you've been unhappy with me for years. Even if I could love you again, I can't change who I am. As soon as I can make the arrangements, I'm going back to my team." My chair makes a loud scraping noise when I push away from the table.

I go to my room, pack up her things, and set them at her feet. She's not moved from the table. "You won't be able to live on base anymore. I'll pay for a hotel room for you until you find a place to live. I'm assuming you'll go back to Asheville. I'll send the rest of your things there when you text me your address."

She sniffs a few times and picks up her bags. "Goodbye, Thorn."

I walk her to the door and watch her pull out of the driveway. I close my eyes and try to remember the girl that I fell in love with all those years ago. She's not the same, and neither am I. I know I told her that I don't love her anymore, but it's a lie I'm telling myself to push her away. She hates this life, and she shouldn't be forced to stay. I'll never make her happy being away, and I can't be here any longer.

CHAPTER 7

THIS CAN'T HAPPEN EITHER

"Why can't you sign my paperwork so that I can get back to my team?" I push the papers across her desk to her.

"That's not how this works. You've been through an ordeal, and I need to make sure you're fit to go back." Dr. Ruth picks up the papers, placing them in a file.

"I'm sure I'm not the only soldier that's been cheated on while overseas. I promise you, I'm fine."

She rests back in her chair. "Have you processed what happened between the two of you?"

"That's a no-brainer, Doc. She never wanted me in the military, and I forced her hand. I thought she'd come around, but she was always afraid I'd never come back. I guess my downfall was that I loved my team more than my wife. I can't blame her for needing more from her husband."

"Sounds like you weren't a fit from the start."

"She was my first girlfriend." I blink my eyes to hold off tears.

"I'm sorry. We never truly forget our first loves. Most people just don't marry them. I am sorry she hurt you."

I lean my elbows on my knees. "Maybe I should suck it up and forgive her and retire."

"Is that what you really want?"

I sigh. "No. I'm a soldier, always will be. I guess that means I'll be alone the rest of my life, other than my brothers in arms."

"It's a hard life to maintain a marriage and a family in, but it can be done with the right person."

I stand. "So, what do you say into letting me go back?"

"I'd like to keep you stationed here for the next month. I'm sure it will take you that long to transfer anyway. Why not have someone to talk to while you're still here?"

She makes me want to stick around. She's easy to talk to, and maybe it will help me get rid of some of the anger that I'm feeling. "Okay."

"I want to see you three days a week." She opens her calendar.

"Damn. Am I that fucked up?" I chuckle.

"There are lots of criteria we can go over before you head back to your SEAL duties. I'd like to discuss your past experiences too."

"Can we meet somewhere other than this office? It's depressing and reminds me of Eden."

"I'm sure that can be arranged." She smiles, and I realize how beautiful she is.

"How about the Mexican restaurant on base? You do like Mexican food?"

"It's my favorite." She pushes a blonde strand of hair behind her ear. For the first time, I notice how green her eyes are. They're beautiful, and a man could easily get lost in them.

"Text me when and where. I'll be there."

* * *

Over the next several weeks, Dr. Ruth and I've spent a lot of time together. One hour bled into the next. We've become comfortable with one another and found that we have a lot in common. Lauryn is smart, sexy, and once you get to know her, she's funny. She's focused on furthering her career in the military. She wants to one day be stationed with a SEAL team. She feels that being able to tune into specific soldiers, she'd be of more help. She graduated a year ago and enlisted right away.

I've filed for a divorce, but Eden is resistant. She keeps calling me every night, begging me to work it out with her. I feel a huge burden of guilt. I hate what she did, but I love her enough to let her go find happiness, knowing it will never be with me.

Lauryn is helping me work through it. She seems to understand that being a soldier is built into my DNA, and it's not something I can willingly change. And honestly, I don't want to.

"You look nice," I say, pulling out Lauryn's chair. We've become regulars at the Mexican restaurant. She's dressed in a light floral dress and a pair of sandals. More comfortable than her usual look.

"Thank you." She sits, and rubs her lips together, smearing the gloss I don't think I've seen her wear before.

"How are you? Did you get anywhere with Eden on the divorce papers?"

"Always directly to the point." I chuckle.

She bites at her lip. "It's not for the reasons you think."

"What do you mean?"

"I know it's wrong, but I have feelings for you that I shouldn't have. We've grown so close over the last couple weeks, and I know I should keep it professional, but every time I'm around you, I want more."

Wow, she's blown me out of the water. I know how attracted I am to her, but I've been brushing it off. I lean close and place my hand on her thigh under the table. "I've been feeling the same way."

She presses a soft kiss to my lips, and it stirs something inside me that I've never felt, not even with Eden. "How about we skip dinner and go back to my place?"

"I'd like that." A sexy smile plays on her face.

I stand and pull her chair out. Her hand folds into mine, and we get in my truck. She slides to the middle, slipping her hand on my leg. I'm instantly hard. The ride across the base is short, and I can feel the intensity building between us.

I unlock the door, and our bodies crash together before it's even closed. Our hands are all over each other, ripping our clothes off so we can touch one another.

"Damn, you're beautiful." I pick her up and carry her to my bedroom. We spend the next several hours enjoying one another. She falls asleep, and I hold her in my arms. My thoughts are racing all over the place. I feel like I've cheated on my wife, but I don't regret a minute of my time with Lauryn.

"You're thinking loudly," she whispers and rolls over into my chest.

"You know this doesn't change anything about me leaving."

"Yes. We'll enjoy each other while you're here and then I'll let you go. We both have career paths to follow, and neither one of us wants to sacrifice that." She slides over the top of me. Her naked core is pressed into mine. I place my hands on her stomach and move them upward to behind her neck. I draw her down to my mouth and kiss her.

"I like the sound of enjoying each other."

This time when she falls asleep, I do too, with her held tightly against me. I wake the next morning to an empty bed.

"Lauryn?"

I hear a noise in the other room then she pokes her head inside. "I'm sorry. You were sleeping so peacefully, I didn't want to wake you. I've got an appointment this morning, and I really need to change clothes before I go to my office."

I throw the covers off and get out of bed. She

meets me halfway. I hug her to my naked body. "Thank you for last night. Will I see you again later?"

"You're welcome and most definitely." She smacks a kiss to my lips. "Text me later."

CHAPTER 8

TIME TO LEAVE

We've spent every spare minute together for the past month. I leave to go back to my unit in two days. We've talked about it and where that leaves us. We're both good with seeing each other when I'm back in the States and nothing more in between. I'll miss her friendship and her body next to mine, but I'll be doing what I was born to do, and so will she. I love the freedom our relationship gives one another.

"I've got a debriefing today, and I won't be home till late tonight," I tell her as I wrap a towel around her wet body.

"How about I pick us up some dinner, and I'll meet you back here. We can get dirty again."

"I love showering with you," I say, kissing her collarbone.

"Thorn! Are you here!"

Eden's voice echoes through the house. "Shit! Stay in here. I'll go see what she wants." I drape a towel around my waist and rush out the door to see her standing in my doorway with papers in her hand.

"You can't just come in my house anytime you want, Eden."

"I knew if I asked, you'd tell me no. I wanted to go over our divorce papers. I know you're leaving soon." She looks around my room.

I should've changed the locks on the door. "Let me get dressed. I'll meet you in the living room."

She turns around like she's going to walk out then spins in my direction. "Is there a woman in here?" She points to Lauryn's purse that's on the nightstand.

"That's none of your business." I walk toward her.

"We're still married."

"Only on paper."

"How is what you're doing any different than what I did?" She's in my face.

"We are not together anymore. We're living separate lives."

"We were living separate lives when I cheated on you."

"It's not the same, and you know it."

"I don't want a divorce, Thorn. You can call us even now, and we can start over."

"Why? Nothing has changed. I'm a SEAL, and you hate it. I'm not giving it up."

She reaches up and touches my face. "I'll take whatever I can get from you. I love you. You promised to love me in good and bad times. Doesn't that commitment mean anything to you?"

"It did until you decided to let another man touch you. You broke our vows, not me."

"I was wrong, and I know that now. I can be a SEAL's wife if you just give me another chance."

"You need to let this go." I walk over to my dresser and pull on a pair of jeans. "I don't want to worry about a wife back home while I'm thousands of miles away."

"Who is she?" She points to the bathroom door.

"You need to leave." I deepen my voice.

"You don't want me because you've found someone else." She scoots by me and rushes to the door, flinging it open. Her eyes grow large when she sees Lauryn wrapped in a towel.

"You! You did this! You were supposed to help us

fix our marriage." She gasps. "You told him about the baby on purpose so you could have him for yourself!"

"That's not true," Lauryn defends herself.

I place my hands on Eden's shoulders, and she jerks away from me. She rips up the divorce papers.

"What are you doing?"

"If you force me to divorce you, I'll expose her. She was our therapist. I'm sure it would ruin her career and more than likely yours."

She heads out the door, and I follow her. "What is it you want from me?"

"I want you to be my husband. Stay here, and we'll work it out. Cancel your transfer. I'm not really asking. You no longer have a choice."

I grab her elbow. "Don't do this, Eden. Don't ruin all our lives."

"I want one year. If during that time, you and I can't work things out, I'll let you go."

"Don't do it, Thorn." Lauryn's voice is behind me.

I turn toward her. "I won't let her ruin you."

"But she'll ruin you." Her tears flow.

"How sweet," Eden snarls.

I whip back in her direction. "One year. You'll only have me by the balls for that long. I will go back to being a SEAL."

"We'll see about that. The other stipulation is that she transfer out of here, and you never see her again."

"I'll transfer, but don't do this to him. It's not going to make him love you again. He'll only learn to hate you." Lauryn is by my side.

"I'll give you a year, but you'll give me something in return."

"What?" She throws a hand on her hip.

"After the year is over, you'll agree to have our marriage records disappear. None of it ever happened. I want it wiped out. You'll get no part of me ever again, including any financial support."

"I can live with that because you'll fall in love with me again, and it will be like she never happened."

"She's insane." Lauryn tugs at my arm. "This isn't about love. It's about punishing you for leaving her. You can't agree to any of this."

I move her out of earshot of Eden. "I'm not letting her destroy you. Your license will be revoked, and everything you're worked for will be gone."

"She's taking everything you've accomplished and discarding it. There has to be more that she wants, and I'm betting it has to do with money."

"It's one year of my life. I'll survive, but if she exposes our affair, you'll have nothing left."

"Do we have a deal or not?" Eden is impatient.

"You'll agree to my terms, and you'll leave Lauryn alone?"

She looks Lauryn up and down. "Yes."

"Then we have a deal."

CHAPTER 9

YEARS LATER

It's her. I haven't seen her since the day she left my place all those years ago. She looks a little older but still as sexy. She's trying not to look at me across the table. I need to focus on Captain Rebel's report and introductions, but damn. My body heated up the moment I laid eyes on her. I've often wondered what happened to her. Did she marry? Obviously, she furthered her career like she wanted.

That year of my life was a living hell. Eden tried everything to make me fall in love with her again, but I'd grown to almost hate her. I had to fight like hell to get back into my unit when the year was over. Eden held up her end of the bargain and never reported Lauryn. She signed the papers, and I had all our records removed. I gave her a lump sum of monies that I felt I owed her, but the papers have now been sealed and she'll never get another dime from me.

I've lived my life since then with one sole purpose in mind, and that's being the best damn soldier that I could be. I've trained and survived many missions. I was transferred here because of a skill set that's needed to protect us on our own soil. Captain Rebel has a good reputation as a leader, and I'm honored to be serving with a SEAL like him.

He calls the meeting after Drake rushes out. I follow Lauryn into the stairwell. "I had no idea you were here," I say as soon as the door shuts behind us.

"I saw your name on the docket, and I let someone else step in and do your in boarding," she says in a hushed voice.

"You didn't have to do that." I take a long look at her. "It's good to see you again."

"I'm sorry about what happened between us and that you sacrificed so much."

"I'm not. I will never be sorry for the time we spent together."

"Eden kept her word?"

"Yes, she's been out of the picture for a long time. How about you? Did you ever marry?"

"No. I've stayed focused on my career."

"Me too." I can feel the heat moving between us.

"You and I need to stay in the past." She licks her lips.

I know she wants me as much as I want her at this very moment. I dip down and capture her lips with mine. She gives in for a brief second then places her hand in the middle of my chest.

"We can't. I'm the therapist for the Gunners. I've worked long and hard to get this job, and I love it. I won't risk it for any feelings I still have for you after all this time."

"We're older and much wiser. We could hide it. I'm still a SEAL and don't want anything to interfere with that either. You could assign me to an outside therapist."

"No. Whatever you and I had in the past is better left there."

"We've been in the same room for less than five minutes, and it's obvious to me that that's not true."

"It was a momentary lapse of weakness. It won't happen again."

I watch her march up the stairs. She looks at me before she opens the door. "I'll expect you to keep your appointments with me professional."

I move up toward her. "Then don't look at me like you want to devour me, sweetheart, because I'd be more than willing to oblige you." I pull the handle on the door and hold it open for her.

"That's not what I was doing," she protests.

I shut the door and press her body up against it. "Every inch of you was screaming it. Your breath increased, your nipples hardened, and I'm betting if I touched you, you'd be wetter than hell," I whisper against her neck, and I feel her swallow.

"It doesn't matter how my body reacts to yours, you have to let this go. Please, I'm begging you."

I inhale sharply, taking a step back. "We'll play this your way, but if you change your mind, you know where to find me."

NINA PAX

Nina Pax
Ekko

CHAPTER 1

NINA - AGE 10

"Make that damn baby quit crying." Mommy lifts her head off the bed. Her hair is matted to her face, and she's in the same clothes from two days ago.

"There's no more formula, and she's hungry." I try to hush her. "I'm hungry too," I whine and know that it makes Mommy mad. I haven't eaten since school on Friday. The cafeteria lady gives me left-overs from lunch to bring home. I give them to Mommy when she wakes up in the morning. It's my favorite time of day with her. Sometimes she feels sorry for me and takes me to eat pancakes.

I love pancakes.

Morning is the only time she's like her old self, but it never lasts long. By midday, she's looking for her drugs. Daddy brings them home, and I become invisible again. I try to make them happy, but I never do.

Mommy crawls out of bed. I think she's going to give me a few dollars to get some food for the baby. She wobbles over to me and swings her arm back. *Smack.*

I cry from the sting to my face. "I told you not to whine about food. And make that baby shut up!" She slams the bathroom door.

"I'm sorry, Rella." I kiss the top of her head. Mommy and Daddy have ignored her since the day Momma had her right here in our trailer. They didn't even give her a name, so I named her Cinderella. On one of Momma's better days, before she had her, she brought home a grocery bag of formula and several boxes of diapers.

I carry Rella over to the bed where Daddy is still sleeping, and I shake his shoulder. "Daddy, Daddy, can I have some money for the baby?" He doesn't move, and he smells.

I peek out the broken blinds. It's almost dark outside. I don't like going out by myself, but Rella doesn't look good. She's not fat like other babies I've seen. Sometimes she's too weak to even cry.

I wrap her in one of Momma's T-shirts and open

the front door. Mommy comes out of the bathroom. "I'm scared. Will you go with me?" I beg her.

She shoos me away with her hand. "You're a big girl. Ain't nobody going to take the likes of you. Don't come back if that baby is still crying."

I walk the dirt road of the trailer park. No one ever speaks to me. I'm invisible to them too. My arms hurt from carrying Rella into town. I always like the dumpster by the fire department. They throw the bones of the pizza away. I don't mind that it's not much, but I'd sure like a taste of the rest of the pizza.

There won't be anything in the dumpster that Rella can eat, so I'll have to go to the store first. I wait until the lady out front isn't looking before I go inside. I tiptoe over to the bottle of milk and tuck two into the T-shirt with Rella. When the lady is busy, I sneak back out.

I sit on the curb around the corner from the store and open a bottle. Rella makes slurping noises and gulps it down. "I'm sorry, baby. I'll find a way to get you some more food." I kiss her tiny nose.

The door to the fire station opens, and a man tosses a pizza box in the dumpster. My mouth waters, I'm so hungry. I carry Rella over to the dumpster and lay her on the sidewalk and climb inside. It always smells so bad, and there are all kinds of bugs.

I hate bugs.

I hear the door open again, and I duck down inside.

"Who do we have here?" a man asks.

I look over the top to see him picking up the baby. I'm so scared, my words don't come out.

He looks around the area. "Don't you worry, little one. I'll take care of you." He kisses the top of her head, and her little hand grasps his finger.

I should say something, but maybe he'll take care of her. Mommy and Daddy don't. I could go with him, but they need me. Mommy would never eat if it wasn't for me.

The man hollers for someone to come outside. Two other men come through the door. He shows them Rella. "I think we should take her to the hospital. She's so tiny and lethargic."

"Where did she come from?" one of them asks.

"She was on the sidewalk when I came outside."

"Someone left her here. It's our job to take care of her."

I watch as they load her in a red truck and drive off. "You'll be okay now, Rella." I open the pizza box and eat all but two bones. I'll save those for later.

My long, tangled, dirty hair gets caught in a crack of the dumpster as I climb out. "Ouch!" I pull hard, and a long strand comes out. I run as fast as I can home. Mommy and Daddy are asleep when I make it back. I pick up their needles and plastic bands and throw them in a bucket.

I curl up in my ragged clothes and lie down on the wood pallet I have for a bed. Momma threw a blanket on it to make it softer, and I found a torn pillow in a neighbor's tin garbage can.

I don't sleep much thinking about Rella. I miss her already, but at least those nice men will take good care of her. She'll be happy, and Mommy won't yell at me anymore that she has too many mouths to feed.

When I wake up in the morning, they're still sleeping. I get in the shower and make sure to only turn on the cold water like I've been told.

I hate cold water.

I use Mommy's brush, and it pulls my hair. Maybe she'll be in a good mood this morning and brush it for me. She always makes it look pretty.

"Wake up!" Mommy screams. "Wake up!"

I run out to her room, and she's shaking Daddy.

"He wouldn't wake up for me last night, either," I tell her.

She curls in a ball and starts crying. I climb up in bed with her. "It's okay, Mommy." I brush her hair.

"He's gone," she cries. "He ain't waking up."

I scoot close to her. "It's okay. I'll take care of us."

She looks up. "Where's your sister?"

"I was climbing into the dumpster at the firehouse to look for some food. I couldn't hold her and get in, so I laid her on the ground. A nice man came out and picked her up. He took her to the doctors."

"It's just as well. She's better off." She lays her head back down, crying, and never mentions the baby again.

CHAPTER 2

NINA - AGE 13

"Momma, you home?" I yell as I come through the front door, which is hanging off its hinges.

A man comes out of her room, buckling up his pants. "She's in there." He points then throws some cash on the counter. I stand to the side and let him walk by me and don't say a word until he's gone.

I grab a twenty-dollar bill off the pile and stuff it in my bra. "Momma, you okay?" I open the door to her room. She's pulling on a pair of jeans and puffing on a cigarette.

"Things are going to get better around here, Nina. I promise."

She tells me that at least once a week. "I made all

As on my report card." I pull it out of my backpack. "My teacher says I have a bright future."

"Keep dreaming, little girl. You ain't getting out of this place. You think you're so much better than me."

Her mood went from pleasant to mean. "I didn't say that, but I want to go to college one day."

"You can get that out of your head right now. I'm not spending any of my hard-earned money on a college education for you."

I've learned to bite my tongue; otherwise she'll start swinging a belt.

"I need some new clothes for a man I'm meeting tonight. Why don't you go down to the laundry mat and pick out something pretty for me?"

Momma thinks the local laundromat is a department store. I got tired of being teased at school about my clothes. They were either dirty or too big. I found a couple quarters on the ground one day and decided to go clean them in a real washer instead of in the sink with soap. That's when I learned that people leave their clothes there and go shopping while they wash or dry them. I started going through them to find some pretty things to fit me. Then Momma made me start stealing them for her too.

The kids at school still make fun of me, but I don't care anymore. I stay to myself most of the time. I'd never fit in, so what would be the point. Instead, I found myself going to the local library after school. The first time I went, I didn't know the books were free as long as you checked them out and brought them back. I stuffed a bunch in my backpack, and the librarian stopped me before I made it out the door, explaining to me that I had to log them out first. She was sweet and kind and seemed to sense that I was sad and lonely. She gave me a journal and told me to write in it every day, that it would make me feel better. I went back as long as I could remember and wrote everything in it.

It didn't make me feel better.

Yet, I still do it.

The only person that's ever nice to me, doesn't speak to me. I'm not sure he talks at all. He lives in the same trailer park as me at the very end of the road. People are always pulling up to his trailer and handing his father an envelope. He hands them something in return, and they drive off. I'm sure they are selling drugs. But the little boy stays to himself. He always smiles at me when he sees me. Somehow, I think he has it worse than I do. He's a cute little kid under all the dirt on his face and clothes.

"Hurry up. He'll be here in a couple hours, and I

want to look pretty for him. Maybe he'll be your new daddy."

I turn around before I roll my eyes. She says that a lot too. This run-down trailer has been a revolving door since Daddy died. She tried to get a real job, but she kept herself so strung out, she'd get fired within the first couple of weeks.

I collect bottles and cans from the neighborhood and take them to the recycling center to get cash. It's enough that I don't go hungry anymore.

I hop on my bike I bought at a thrift store and go into town. I ride slow every time I go by the firehouse. I often think of Rella and hope that she found a good home. I do my usual thing and wait for the laundromat to clear out, other than an old man that's always sleeping in the corner. I quickly go through the dryers and stuff clothes in my bag and ride home.

"I stole you a pretty blue dress." I'm taking it out of my backpack as I walk in the door.

She snatches it out of my hand. "That is nice. It'll match my blue eyes."

Momma's eyes are brown, at least that's the way they always look. Her eyes are so dilated from the drugs and being inside.

"I want you gone by the time he gets here." She pulls the dress over her head.

I'll go to my usual spot and read about things I can only dream of. The library stays open until eight, but the librarian lets me stay until she's ready to walk out the door.

I get back on my bike and go into town. When I walk in, there are several kids that are in my class, sitting at a table together. They snicker and whisper at me when I walk by. I square my shoulders and don't pay any attention to them. I get lost in a book for several hours before the librarian tells me it's time to go.

I ride home in the dark. There's a big black pickup truck parked outside. I'm tired and want to go straight to bed, so I tiptoe inside, trying not to disturb Momma. I've graduated from a pallet to a stinky old twin mattress. I think someone died on it. It smells awful.

I hate it.

I change into my pajamas and lie down. As soon as I do, the bedroom door opens, and Momma walks out, smiling.

"Who is this?" The man's voice is gruff. He wipes his chin with his hand.

"My daughter Nina." Momma straightens her dress.

"She's a pretty little thing."

His words make my stomach ache.

"You like her?" Momma pulls me off the bed with her hand.

"She's got a tight little body." He's eyeing me up and down, making me feel uncomfortable.

"For an extra two hundred dollars, she's yours for the rest of the night." My mom holds her hand out.

"What? No!" I jerk out of her grasp.

He pulls cash from his pocket.

"I'm not for sale!" I cry.

"You'll do as you're told. You're old enough to help make some money to help pay the bills." She points at me, snarling.

"You mean to help you buy drugs. I won't do it!" I scream and head for the front door. His large hand reaches out and catches me by the hair, yanking me backward.

"Let go of me!" I yell and try to free myself from him. His grip is so hard, a handful of hair is ripped from my head.

"Oww! Please stop!" I can't help but cry it hurts so bad.

He drags me by the hair back to Momma's room and slams the door, whipping his belt from its loops. He's too big and strong for me to fight him.

CHAPTER 3

NINA - AGE 17

"Nina, your grades are so good you can get into any college that you want. You made a perfect score on your SAT's."

"I'm not going to college, Mrs. Gary," I tell my guidance counselor.

"Why not? You're one of the smartest young ladies I've ever had at this school. Why wouldn't you want to go to college?"

"It's not that I don't want to." I bite my bottom lip and wring my hands together. "My mother can't afford to send me to school."

"You'll get a full-ride scholarship with your grades and additional monies from the state based on your family's income. Have your mother and father come in, and I can discuss it with them."

I want to tell her my father's been dead for years, but I don't. My mother has never stepped foot in school. I've always lied and told them she was too busy with her job as a dancer. I've gotten good at telling lies and putting on masks.

It's taken me a long time to figure out how to fit in; my mask makes it so much easier. I put it on, and people see me. I've learned to be fake enough to fit in and make a few friends. Well, they aren't really my friends.

I hate all of them.

But pretending has made my life more bearable. I can stay out late at a so-called friend's house and not have to deal with the men my mother has over, or her all-night, drug-induced binges. I spend all my time studying, finding ways to earn money, and cleaning our shithole of a trailer. The roof leaks every time it rains, and it smells like sex and cigarettes.

Mom still sells me out to her men friends. That's when a different mask goes on. A colder one filled with indifference and defiance.

I loathe the mask.

When the door is closed, I demand more money and tell them the deal is off if they tell my mother they gave me more. It works every time. I've got a stash of money hidden in a can underneath the trailer.

Men disgust me. Even the ones I think might be nice.

I hate all men.

"Nina?"

Mrs. Gary's voice brings me out of my fog.

"Do you think you could get your parents in here?"

"They're too busy. If you give me the information, I'll go over it with them."

She hands me the application and flyers. "There is a deadline. You'll need to have these back to me in a couple of weeks, along with the application fee of two hundred dollars."

"I thought you said I'd have a full ride?"

"You will, but you have to pay these fees."

"Thank you, Mrs. Gary." I stuff them in my bag.

"Let me know if you need anything. I could come to your house to talk to them if you want."

"No, that's okay. They are both away on a business trip. I'll call them tonight." I rush out the door before she asks me any more questions.

When I make it home, one of her regulars is pulling out of the dirt driveway. I walk in, and Mom is rolling up her sleeve, tapping the inside of her arm.

"I'm surprised you have any veins left," I say, throwing my bag on the couch.

"Don't talk to me like I'm a piece of trash," she snarls.

I want to tell her if the shoe fits. "I just met with the guidance counselor at school. I earned a perfect score on my college entrance exams. She said I could go to whatever college I wanted, and it would be paid for."

"You ain't going nowhere. I'm sure there was some screwup. You ain't smart enough to amount to anything."

Another mask goes into place. The one where I pretend her words don't hurt me. I'm either stupid or ugly. Those are the mild words she's called me through the years.

"I found that dumb journal you've been keeping."

The hair on my arms raise. "What do you mean, you 'found it?'"

"As in I read all the crap you've been writing. Half that stuff ain't true."

"How would you know? You're too drugged out to know the truth."

She jumps out of her chair, and I protect my face with my hands. "Why you ungrateful bitch!"

"Ungrateful? I've been the one taking care of you all these years. I've done unspeakable things to keep this shithole over our heads and food on the table. You spend every dime you make on drugs. You couldn't care less about me. I'm only good to clean up your mess."

"Don't you dare disrespect me like that!" She raises her hand to slap me. Instead of cowering, I face her and straighten my shoulders.

"I disrespected you a long time ago. When you didn't give a shit that Rella was gone."

"Who the hell is Rella?"

I laugh. "My sister. You've never even talked about her once since that day." I refuse to cry.

"I never wanted her in the first place. She would've been one more thing for me to take care of."

"Thing!" I scream. "She was your daughter, not a thing! You never wanted me either!"

She falls on the couch and starts tapping her arm again. "That's not true. Your daddy and I both wanted you."

"Yeah, until the two of you got hooked on drugs. The same drugs that took his life."

She holds a small bag out to me. "Do you want some? Do you have any idea how amazing they make you feel?"

"I know what they've done to your life and mine. Who do you think has put you back together all these years? I want nothing to do with that shit." I smack the bag from her hand.

"You bitch!" She scrambles to get if off the floor. "I'll make sure you don't go anywhere. I'll call the cops and tell them you're the one who's been stealing stuff from the local stores."

I pick up the phone that's been disconnected for years. "Call them. I'll tell them how you've been selling your daughter all these years."

She straps the band around her arm.

"Where is my journal?" I seethe.

"In the trash, where it belongs. That's where I should've put your baby sister when she was born."

Her words trigger a deep hate inside me, and I snap. It's a darkness I can't control. "Do you want help with that?" I point to her needle.

She smiles and holds it out.

I draw up the liquid and get the air out of the syringe. I've got tons of experience on how to do this and the exact amount she needs. She holds out her arm, and I inject it. Within seconds, her head falls back, and her eyes roll.

"That's my girl," she slurs.

I draw up more, and when she's completely out of it, I inject into the crook of her arm.

* * *

A handful of people are at the gravesite. My mother didn't have any friends. A few of my teachers, the librarian, my guidance counselor, and my fake friends stand beside me, as I yet again wear another mask. The grieving one. I play the part well.

I hate crying.

After the small funeral, my counselor pulls me aside. "Why didn't you tell anyone about your family situation?"

I have to work hard to force tears out. "I was ashamed and didn't want anyone to know." I cry on her shoulder.

"Do you have any other family to stay with until you graduate?"

"I'll be fine. I've been taking care of myself for years."

"You really should live with someone."

"I'll be eighteen in two weeks and a legal adult." I sniff and dab my eyes with a tissue.

"If you need anything, you have my number."

"Thank you. I appreciate it. I'll have my application on your desk in the morning."

"Any idea where you want to go to college?"

"Harvard. I want to study physics with a minor in business."

CHAPTER 4

NINA - AGE 26

College classes were a breeze for me. I did nothing but study and avoided making any relationships. I didn't join a sorority or hang out with the girls that did. I sat in the back of the classroom, going unnoticed like when I was a kid. Except, this was by choice.

I took a part-time job at a laboratory that studied DNA. Every dime I made, I invested in the company that ended up becoming a national lab for genetic testing. After I graduated, I took a full-time job and became the vice president of the company. The president was a man named Bradley West. He was in his late forties, married, and cheated on his wife almost daily. His swinging door reminded me of my mother's.

I dislike him immensely, but he's a means to an end for me. He has important connections that I need to start out on my own. Government contracts through the military are profitable. With my science and business expertise, I want to branch out to make foreign connections. My only goal in life is to have so much money that I will never have to be poor again. I'm talking billions. I want a life that most people can never achieve, homes all over the world, fancy cars, nice clothes, and the ability to eat at the most expensive restaurants in the world.

I don't fool myself into thinking I was born to help feed the world or be a humanitarian of any kind. I'm in it for myself and no one else. I don't ever want to get married or have children. I had my tubes tied as soon as I graduated college. No mistakes for me. My eye is on the prize. I don't need, nor do I want a man.

My masks have changed since I was a girl. I have what I call the mask of pleasure. Since I want no ties, I wear it when I get the urge to have sex. Men are so easy. I prefer the married ones. That way, they run back to their wives at the end of the day.

The other mask I wear is when I need to play well with others to get what I want. That one, I don't mind so much because it's useful in manipulating investors. They all see me as someone who has her shit together. A past without issues. I'm well respected among my colleagues and the board of directors. They see who I want them to see.

Today, I want them to see a smart business-woman with a plan. My black heels click on the tile floor as I make my way into the boardroom. A team of twelve men is waiting on me, and I'm betting nearly every one of them has a boner at the sight of me.

"I'll get straight to the business at hand." I toss a stack of papers on the oval table. "I want to expand this company's business into organ procurement. It's the next likely step for DNA testing."

"Let me stop you right there," Bradley says, tugging at his tie. "You and I've already discussed this at length. This is not something this company needs to take on, nor do we want to in the near future. We've made millions and don't need to expand."

I sit on the edge of the table. "Millions is enough for you? We could be making billions. Why sell out short?"

"I wouldn't call it selling out. This company is successful because we've focused on one thing. We're the best at what we do, and organ procurement has some ethical issues behind it. I don't want any bad publicity for the company I've built."

"Yes, and part of that is because of me. I pushed you to hire the best in the world and purchased top-rated equipment. The research I've brought into this company alone is part of its success." I get up and pace around the board members. "There is so much more we can do with this company."

The older man sitting next to Bradley leans over and says something in his ear. "I understand," he says to him, then squares his shoulders at me. "That is not the direction we are taking this company." His voice is stern.

"Then you have my resignation, and I'll be cashing in all of my stock, which will bring this company down to its knees."

"That's not necessary." Bradley stands. There's no need to cash out."

I walk over to him and lightly tap his cheek. "There's no need for me to stay funded in a company that doesn't want to grow. I'll take my money and go elsewhere." I can hear the roaring of their voices as I walk out of the room and shut the door.

They have no vision.

I'll use my connections and chart my own path. A path that includes one day finding my sister.

* * *

Six years later...

"Mr. Bari, it's so nice to meet you." I bow. I've been working on this meeting for a long time. I've studied Afghanistan, weaponry, tactical skills, and the wealth of his family. He has a wife and a nineteen-year-old son whom he's been grooming for years. He's my way into building all the cash I need to fund my next project.

"I'm not in the habit of doing business with woman." His English is broken as he sits at the small table in the back of a run-down restaurant in the middle of his town.

"Don't think of me as a woman, but a business partner. I have the means to expand your company into the US market." I open a folder I brought with me and lay it out in front of him. "I've purchased this port in Seattle. I own all the boats and equipment. I also own the men that allow for import and exports in this region." I point on the map.

"You can move fifty percent of my drugs through this port?" He raises an eyebrow.

"Yes, without being caught."

"I'll give you my business on one condition."

"Name it."

"The military in this area is trying to take me down. I need protection. My home is well hidden, and I need it to stay that way. If I don't have poppy fields, there is nothing to sell. My men have been able to protect me so far, but US intelligence keeps snooping around."

"You want me to misdirect them?" I have men in place to run the port out of Seattle. I could contract with the military. I know all the ins and outs of this area, and with my knowledge, I could be a military handler, easily.

"Yes."

"There has to be more in it for me?"

"What is it that you want?"

"Not only do I want fifty percent of your business coming through me, I want ownership in your poppy fields."

He scratches his chin. "Ten percent."

"Twenty-five."

"No deal."

I take out another map and pin my finger to a spot on it. "This is your home. I can lead them right to you." He goes to say something, and I stop him. "Before you threaten to kill me, these records are in a safe with instructions upon my death to be opened and sent to our military leaders."

"You leave me no room for negotiations."

"No."

He laughs. "I like you. You're intelligent and greedy, like me. We have a deal."

"Not so fast, there's more."

"What more could you want from me?" He slams his fist on the table.

"I know about your other dirty work."

"How do you know about that?"

"I'm a woman with lots of connections."

"I will not give you any part of it." He stands, and the table moves.

"I don't want money. I want you to teach me the ins and outs of trafficking young women."

He sits. "Why would a woman like you want to know such things?"

"Because I have bigger plans."

"Do tell, Ms. Pax."

"Procuring human organs and selling them to the highest bidder. I do believe you'd be in the market for my knowledge."

"You're as evil as I am." He chuckles.

"You have no idea. Do we have a deal or not?"

"I believe we do."

CHAPTER 5

BECOMING AN EKKO

Afghanistan is hotter than hell. I don't know how these military men wear full uniforms. I settled in a week ago, but haven't left the debriefing area. Commander Lukas is in charge of directing SEAL team six, aka the Gunners. He's tough and intelligent, but not enough to see through my lies. I'm better at this game than anyone else. He has no idea that I led the other SEAL team into an ambush. They were getting too close to Bari, so they had to be eliminated. Then they reassigned Bari to the Gunners. I transferred here when I got word of it.

Teaming with Bari and the profits I'm making hand over foot are worth a few soldiers' lives.

My mask has grown thicker.

In my spare time, I've been working out for the

past year. I've toned down, and my arms are rather shapely. I've not been able to work out for the past week, so my goal today is to find the gym in this godforsaken place.

I slip on a white tank top and a gray pair of shorts, pulling my mocha-colored hair into a pony, and head out of my barracks to find the mock gym. I locate it across from the mess hall. When I open the tent, there are ten pairs of eyes on me. I must be the only woman they've seen in a while. I reach for the chin-up bar and start my exercise routine, despite one of the men yelling to a soldier that hasn't taken his eyes off me.

"Rebel, I bet she could outdo you." A soldier laughs, bringing on wagers from the other men.

The big guy gets up and walks over to me. He's sexy as hell with his scruffy face, short dark hair, and bare chest. The look he's giving me is leaving burn marks on my skin. He'd be someone I could have a little fun with in bed. That body of his is to die for.

"I'm Derrick. You must be new here?"

"Are you in charge of these men?" I gaze around the gym.

"You'll have to excuse them. You're the first woman that's stepped inside this place in a good while."

"How much is the bet?"

"They were only teasing. There is no bet." He looks over his shoulder at them.

"A hundred dollars," one of them yells.

"Shut the fuck up, Drake." He snarls.

"I'll take that bet," I say.

"You understand the bet is that you'll beat me in pull-ups." He grins.

I step close enough to breath him in. It's a sexy scent that I want all over me. "Are you afraid?" I stare into his penetrating eyes.

"It's your money." He laughs and positions himself beside me on the bar.

"You ready?" I ask.

"Whenever you are, sweetheart."

No man has ever called me that. I'm anything but sweet.

"I'll count to three," the soldier he called Drake shouts. "One, two, three."

I lift and lower to the bar. I watch him out of the corner of my eye. His biceps bulge with each lift. I've never been so attracted to a man before. I should let him win, but it's not in me. I like the competition.

Sweat is pouring off me, and my arms are burning. He's slowing down. I think I can take him. He groans loud, and I see pain sear his face, but he keeps going. The man is a beast. It takes everything I have to raise myself one more time, hoping he's done. I lower and try to lift again, but can't do it. I fall to the ground with my muscles screaming.

"Damn it, you almost had him." Drake runs over to my side.

"I wasn't going to let a woman beat me." Derrick lets go of the bar and holds his bicep.

Now, he's just being a jerk. I swat Drake away from me and get off the ground. "Well, this woman was close to kicking your ass."

"How about a peace offering?" Derrick asks.

I wipe the sweat off my forehead. "What did you have in mind?" I know what I'd like from him. My gaze travels up and down his hot body.

"A cold beer. We have the best cantina around." His smile is broad.

"It's the only cantina in town." I flash him a rare grin.

"Fair enough." He chuckles. "Are you game or not?"

Oh, I'm game alright, but not for beer. "Lead the way."

I follow him to a tin building across from the gym. Compared to everything else in this place, it isn't half bad. The bar has a nice shiny piece of oak for a countertop, and it's surrounded by corrugated metal. Strands of lights hang around the edge of the ceiling. Barstools line the edge with a few small tables inside. Half the bar opens up to an outdoor seating area with dartboards and corn hole for entertainment. The only thing not made to look nice is the dusty dirt floor.

"Two cold beers," Derrick tells the soldier behind the bar.

"Don't I get a choice?" I say as he pulls out a barstool for me.

"We only have one brand of beer, so unless you want a liquor drink, of which we're limited too, a cold brew is your only choice."

I watch his muscular frame lean over the bar and grab two glasses. His body warms mine up. Never have I reacted to a man like I do him. He's the type man that could make me forget my own damn name and maybe purpose.

"When did you get here?" He pours the bottle of beer into the glass.

"I've been here a week."

"Funny, I haven't seen you until today." He slides the glass in front of me.

"I've been buried in briefings."

He looks me up and down. "You don't look military."

I pick up my beer and guzzle it half down. "I'm a civilian contractor."

He grins and takes a gulp of his drink. "You the new handler for the Gunners?"

"Let me guess. You're their leader?"

"Captain Derrick Rebel." He puts out his hand for me to shake.

I stare at it, willing it to be all over my body, touching every inch of me. "Nina Pax." I finally meet his hand with mine.

"Ekko," he says, chuckling.

"Excuse me?" My brows dip together.

"You'll be in our ear, so you'll be an Ekko to us."

"I'd prefer Ms. Pax." I take another drink.

"Miss," he repeats.

"Yes, and I plan on keeping it that way."

He sits on the stool. "You just haven't met the right man to sweep you off your feet yet."

"There is no such man. How about you, any Mrs. back home?"

"Never met the right woman." He scans my body. "Where are you from?"

"Where I'm from isn't important, it's where I'm

going that fuels me." I can't believe I told him that. I never talk about myself.

"And, where is it you're headed?"

"To be the best handler," I lie. I'll go down as the worst in history.

"Beyond that?" He angles his body toward me.

"Make a shit load of money." I've never been that honest.

"Really? In this business, that will be hard to do unless you have an in with the men in this country." He sounds serious.

This man is smart. He sees right through me.

He bursts out laughing. "I'm only kidding with you."

I blow out the breath I was holding. "I negotiate my own terms. My knowledge is very valuable to the military. They'll pay me whatever price I ask."

"Confident. I like that in a woman."

Totally out of character for me, I place my hand on his thigh. "I like a man that's a leader."

He inhales deeply. "What would you say to going back to my place to get to know one another better?" He raises a brow.

"I'd say...lead the way, Captain."

CHAPTER 6

HARDER THAN I EVER THOUGHT

Months later...

I wrap my leg around Derrick's hip and press the core of my body into his, making him hard as a rock again despite the fact that he fucked me half the night.

"Baby, you keep that up"—he looks between his legs—"no pun intended, I'll never make the mission."

"God forbid you miss out on one mission." I need to find a way to keep him on base. I unwind my body from his and throw the sheet off as I get out of bed. I give him the perfect view of my ass, and he smiles.

"Come on, Ekko, and bring that fine ass back to bed."

I grimace. "You know I hate that you call me that when we're not at work."

He falls back on the bed with a huff and rubs his hand down his scruffy face. "Nina Pax, would you please crawl back into bed with me?"

I secretly like that he calls me Ekko, but I hate when his men do it. "I can't. I'm going to be late for my meeting with the commander," I say with a mouth full of toothpaste as I wave my pink brush at him.

He groans and lifts his leg up to hike himself off the bed, joining me in the bathroom. "You want me to skip out on a mission, but you're not willing to miss a meeting." He wraps his hands around my naked body and presses his teeth lightly into my shoulder.

I'm tempted to bail on all my contracts and stay right here with this man. I'd give anything for my life to be different, but no matter what I feel for him, I won't let a man become my world. "My life isn't on the line every time I go to work." I lean over the sink and spit out the toothpaste and press my ass into his cock. I can never get enough of him. His hands glide to either side of my hips, then smacks my ass.

"Hey!" I laugh, wanting more. I turn in his arms. "You know how much I like your hands on me, but I really don't have time." I've got a phone call to make. I place a quick kiss to his lips.

He reaches for the shaving cream and lathers it on his face. "When are you ever going to agree to marry me?" He watches my reflection in the mirror as I get dressed in a black suit.

I'd give anything to be normal, take off all my masks, and marry him. "We've talked about this. Neither one of our careers are good on marriages." I have to stay focused on my life's plan.

He looks lost in thought for a moment as he smooths the razor down his handsome face. Shaving cream drips into the sink. "Why don't we both retire then?" he asks nonchalantly.

Would he really give this all up for me? He loves being a SEAL. I sit on the small, rickety bench seat by the closet and slip on a pair of black, shiny heels. "Neither one of us are ready for that. You love your job." No man could love a woman that much.

"I would give it up for you."

I believe he would, but I won't give up millions for him. I don't want to see him physically hurt, but I won't be stopped by his pretty words. I get up and stand beside him, looking at him in the mirror.

"Derrick, I'm not ready to give any of this up. I have some things starting to work for me." Things he can never know about, like my dealings with Bari and the fact that I had the other SEAL team taken out." Things he'd never forgive me for. I wind my hair into a bun.

"I have no idea what that means. Everything you do turns to gold. You've gotten us out of more shit than any other military leader I've had in the past."

That's because I know where Bari's men are. The team hasn't gotten close enough to Bari's location to not protect them until now. It all looks good for me. "My lips are sealed." I smack my lips together to spread my nude-colored lipstick.

"I know, highly classified, need to know only." He rinses off his face and towel dries it before he grabs me. "The only thing I need to know is that you love me." He kisses the tip of my nose.

"You know I do." I do love him. He's become much more than a plaything to me. "Now please take your sexy ass back to bed and skip the mission. Let Captain Stark step in for you today. He's been jonesing to go out on standby for you." *Please, Derrick, I'm begging you. If you don't, you won't make it back alive.*

"Fat chance of that, and let him take all the

glory? These are my men, and the only way I'm not leading them is if I'm six feet under."

An ache like I've never felt before hits me. Six feet under is where he'll likely be if I can't convince him to stay behind. Maybe I can convince Bari's men not to kill him. Either that or I need to back out of my contract to keep him alive. I squeeze my eyes tightly together and press the palm of my hand against my temple. "Ahh...I really gotta go." I turn to leave but glance over my shoulder. "I'll see you in the war room, Rebel." I want to beg him, but I know it won't do any good. I can't manage anything but a frown.

"You okay?" he asks, almost as if he's read my sadness.

"Yeah. Good luck on your mission today." I have to act normal, or he'll see right through me. Why does he have to be so damn smart? I crack open the door and slink out of the barracks. I don't like the men in his platoon knowing about us.

I dial my phone on the way to my meeting. "Alba." I don't like his son, who I've been dealing with since his death. He's more ruthless than his father was and harder to deal with on a business level. He tried to cancel my contracts with him, so I had to blackmail him into honoring them when his father was killed last year, shortly after I met with him.

"I don't want you to kill them, only scare them off," I whisper.

"If they make it within a thousand feet of my home, I'll kill them all. Make no mistake about it."

"Then kill all of them but their leader. Leave him for me," I bark and hang up and head for my meeting with the commander to go over my false intel that is going to lead his men into slaughter.

When he and I are done, I walk into the war room that is filling up with the team. I huddle in the corner with the commander. "What if my intel is wrong?" I need him to back out of this plan.

"So far, your information has been spot on. Why would this be any different? You're the best at what you do, and I trust you."

No one should ever trust me. I don't see a way around this. Rebel walks into the room, and I want to scream that it's a set up. I keep my mouth shut and watch him talk to each of his team members before Commander Lukas draws them together. He calls out the name of each of the team members like he does at every war room meeting. When he's done, I hand him a folder, and he waves it in the air.

"We finally have good intel on the notorious

MM20 group. As you know, this group owns well-guarded poppy fields all over Afghanistan that are supporting their terrorist group with weapons and the ability to go in and out of countries undetected."

Little do any of them know, they are using my port in Seattle.

"They're single-handedly responsible for the last four terrorist attacks in the US, killing over 8,000 men, women, and children. We have a location on where the terrorist cell has been operating out of, thanks to Ms. Pax." He turns toward me.

I think one of Bari's men leaked the location. Someone with an ax to grind. Now, I'm left to clean up their mess.

"Nice job, Ekko," Theo yells out.

I cut my gaze in his directions, and he loses all trace of the smile he was wearing and clears his throat. "Sorry, Ms. Pax."

I pick up a rolled map and lay it out on the table. I'm leading the lambs to the slaughter. "My source tells me that they're hidden in this mountain." I point to an area opposite the poppy fields known location. "He has several smaller cells that guard the fields." I think Bari is trying to cut me out, so maybe I can make this work to my advantage. "Rumor is, he doesn't go anywhere near them. He has a house built into the side of the mountain. Guards protect it twenty-four seven, and the desert area around him is covered in mines." If I let this play out, I can own the poppy fields one hundred percent. I can make this work and keep Derrick safe.

"Who's your source?" Derrick asks.

He knows damn good and well I can't give up a source, or I'll never get more intel. "You know I can't reveal a source."

"How do you know you can trust him? Maybe he's a plant to get us up there?" He leans back in his chair and crosses his arms over his chest. "We've already lost one entire team this year based on bad intel. They were led into a trap and ambushed. I don't want the same for my men."

He suspects something. "And you think I do?" I tap my heel on the ground like I'm pissed.

"I'm not saying that. I only want to make sure that this isn't the same source that had the other SEAL team killed."

I move over and whisper to the commander, "Your team doesn't have as much faith in me as you do."

"This meeting is over for now," he orders. "You men need to go get your gear gathered up and whatever supplies you need to take with you. You'll be leaving in two hours." He gives them instructions on where and when to meet the Blackhawk that will be taking them.

Metal chairs scrape the ground as they get up. Commander Lukas orders Derrick to stay behind. I gather my folders and head out without making eye contact with him. I've got to find another way to keep Derrick from going on this mission. I don't want him killed, and I don't want him finding out that I'm the person behind Bari.

CHAPTER 7

I CAN'T STOP HIM

I march out and head to the cantina to down a beer before I call Bari again. I walk in the alley between two large tents. "They've canceled the mission. You can turn your men back around. No need for them to sit and wait in the mountains for nothing."

"You're lying."

"Why would I lie?" I give him my sincere tone.

"I don't trust you. Never have. I don't know why my father agreed to do business with you."

"Because I made him even richer, and if you were a smart boy, you'd keep your damn mouth shut." My civility with this kid is gone.

"I'll call my men off, but if you're lying, I won't

only kill your captain, I'll kill you too. You need to get here. There's a problem with one of our shipments."

"That's not my problem. It's yours."

"You need to be here by tomorrow."

Rebel is storming toward me. "Alright," I say, hanging up and stuffing the phone in my pocket.

"What's going on here?" Rebel's voice is harsh.

"Nothing to concern you." I don't have time for him; I've got one more trick up my sleeve to prevent him from going on this mission, but I have to work fast. I try to walk by him, but he grabs me by the elbow.

"Look, you can't be angry with me for wanting to protect my men."

The mask of lies goes into place. "Do you think I'd purposely put you in danger?"

"No, but I know how badly you want to capture Abba Bari, and I don't want your ego getting in the way by trusting the wrong person."

He only thinks that because that's what I've made him believe. "My ego? You're the one that has an ego around here. Always disobeying orders. If anyone puts your men in danger, it's you." His ego is what I love most about him.

"I've never lost one man. Wait, is this why you wanted me to bow out of the mission and let someone else take over? You don't like that I don't take orders from you?"

"No, that was not the reason, but maybe you should think about it!" I grit my teeth for effect. *Please think about it, Derrick. I'm not sure any of us are safe.* I scoot by him, and he chases me.

"I'm sorry if I embarrassed you in front of my men, if that's what's pissing you off, but I would've questioned anyone's intel after what happened to the last team. I don't want to send my men home in body bags."

"Are we done here, Captain Rebel? Because I have a lot of things to do to prepare for while our team makes its way to Abba Bari's house."

"Don't be pissed, baby. I hate leaving on a mission with you angry at me."

Don't be sweet to me. "Then you should've thought about that before you started questioning me." I stop and glare at him to make him think I'm really angry at him, when in truth, if I'd pull off my mask, I'd run into his arms and confess everything.

"I wasn't questioning you. I was questioning how reliable your source is."

"It didn't sound that way to me." I defiantly put my hands on my hips.

He wraps his hands through my arms and pulls me to him. "Please don't be angry." He kisses me. It takes everything I have not to give into him.

"I have a lot of work to do." I look past him, and he lets me go. I stomp off but turn around before I make it through the war room door. "Goodbye, Derrick." It's the first time in my life I've regretted leaving any man. I go inside and duck into Commander Lukas's office.

"May I borrow your computer?" I point to it.

He nods

I access Derrick's file and print out what I'm looking for to stop him from this mission. I throw the paperwork on his desk. "Captain Rebel needs to be removed."

"He's the best leader I have. Why would I want to have him stand down?" He flips through the paperwork.

"Keep reading. He's stressed and out of sorts lately."

"I haven't noticed anything different."

"Trust me. He's not the man you want on this mission." I sit across from him and let him read.

"I'll take care of this."

We both get up, and I follow him into the war room where Derrick has a picture of Abba Bari on the screen. I lurk in the back, and Commander joins the men. I watch Derrick as the commander goes over the plan. My heart, that hasn't hurt since the day I left my sister at the fire station, begins to ache. I could confess everything, but it will kill anything Derrick felt for me, so either way, I'll lose him. I might as well keep the ball in my court.

Derrick glances up, and our eyes lock. I lift my chin and look the other way. I can't look him in the eye anymore.

Commander Lukas looks at me, and I nod. "There is one more thing." He turns toward Derrick. "Captain Stark will be leading your men. It has come to my attention that you haven't taken any time off that is required of you."

Derrick glances at me, and I look away again. "I haven't needed the time off, and we've all been putting in extra hours since the other SEAL team was killed, sir."

He states military policy about required time off. The men fight back, telling him if Derrick doesn't lead, then they won't go on the mission.

Commander Lukas is not one to be backed into a

corner. "If your men refuse to go, they'll be pulled from the team."

They all argue back.

"This isn't about what you want, Captain Rebel. It's about you following rules."

Derrick's fist makes contact with the table, causing me to jump. "Everyone out now!" His men scramble. I hustle out with them. I rush back over to the cantina for another beer. I have to stop this. If I do, it will cost me everything I've worked for all these years. I'll still have a few million in the bank, but I'll be in prison, so a lot of good it will do me. I'll go to Bari like he wants and put a bullet in his head. That will stop him, and Derrick will be safe. I rush out into the daylight and lower my sunglasses, but only make it outside the cantina before I have another argument with myself. I lean against the wall and tap my finger to my lips, trying to think of the best plan to keep him safe and still get what I want. I see Derrick heading my way. I push off the wall and start to walk away.

"Wait!" he yells, and I stop dead in my tracks. I shouldn't, I should keep going as fast as I can. "Would you like to explain to me why you don't want me to go on this mission with my men?"

I yank my sunglasses off. "I'm afraid you won't

come back from this one." It's the first truth I've spoken. I cross my arms over my chest and don't realize I'm crying. I've forgotten what it's like to cry. The last time I did, my mother smacked me across the face.

He closes the distance between us. "Why? What makes this one different than any other one I've been on?" I bite my bottom lip, not wanting him to know it's because I don't have his back. "Is it because of the other team? Are you doubting your source now?"

"No. I just know how ruthless Bari is, and if you get caught, he'll kill every one of you."

"And you think I'd let my men risk their lives and I step out of the way? Fuck that, Nina." He braces his strong arm on the wall behind me. "I love you, baby, but don't think for one minute that you'll take this away from me. This is what I do." He places a quick kiss to the side of my face and heads toward his men.

"And this is what I do," I whisper and wipe my tears.

As soon as it's dark, I slip out of the barracks and take a jeep, headed for Bari. I need to get there before the

Gunners. I drive all night and park the jeep a mile outside Bari's place and go in on foot. His men know me, so as soon as I bring down the dark mask I'm wearing, they recognize me, lowering their weapons and escort me into Bari's home hidden in the mountain.

He's briefing a few of his men. When I walk in, they disperse. "I'm glad to see you're capable of following orders." His voice is annoyingly sarcastic.

I could slit his throat, but there are too many of his men here. "Why did you summon me for a problem with a shipment. That's not my end of the deal until the ship arrives in Seattle."

"That's not the real reason I asked you here. I want to purchase your port and wash my hands of you."

"It's not for sale, and if you don't want to continue to do business with me, then I'll find someone else."

I fucking hate him.

I storm out of his house only to hear gunshots ringing out. When I go to step back inside, I hear Derrick's voice telling Bari not to move, or he'll kill him. I listen to their footsteps, walking toward the back of the house. I creek the door open and tiptoe inside. Derrick and Theo have a gun pointed at Bari, and they are going out the secret entrance.

I've got to find a way out of here without being noticed. I open the front door again, and the gunshots are closer. I hear an explosion and cries of agony. I shut the door. I'll have to wait until it's settled down. They won't come back in here; they have who they want. I hear another bomb go off, and soon after, Bari and his men are dragging Derrick and Theo in the door. Derrick is out cold, and his face is covered in blood. Theo is thrown on the floor, and his arm is gone. It's a gory sight like I've never seen.

Bari's men set Derrick in a chair and tie his hands behind his back and bind his legs with a rope. His muddy blood drips down his pant leg. His eye is so swollen, I don't think he'll be able to open it. Theo groans a few times and passes out.

As Derrick starts to stir, I yank his head back by the hair, and Bari points a gun at his head. If I don't act like I'm still on his side, he'll kill me too.

"I see you're still with us, Captain Derrick Rebel." He spits in his face. "So unfortunate for you and your friend."

Derrick tugs at his binds, and I let go of his hair and walk away. I step in the other room and heave several times. I listen to Bari tell Derrick his men are all dead and that no one can stop him.

Derrick tells him he's a sick fuck, and Bari does nothing but laugh.

"You have no idea how powerful I am."

Arrogant little bastard. I should've slit his throat.

"Even the powerful will fall. We took your father out, and you'll be next." Why does Derrick have to taunt him?

Bari tells him he's going to make his death slow and painful. He motions for one of his men armed with a sword and grenades to go to Derrick.

"I made it this far, I deserve to know who tipped you off that we were coming."

Shit. Bari will not hesitate to sell me out. I need to find a weapon to kill him before he does. I quietly move back in his direction. There is a guard only a few feet away from me. I could grab his gun and shoot Bari between the eyes before he even knows what happened.

"You do deserve to know because it will cause you much pain."

The guard moves out of my reach.

"Wait, how did you know my first name was Derrick?"

That's it. He'll expose me. Better I do it myself so

I can save grace with Bari. I'll walk out alive. If I play my cards right, I can get Derrick out of here too. He'll hate me, but at least he'll be alive.

I walk up behind him then stand in front of him.

"Ekko." He swallows hard.

I pull down my mask. "I tried to convince you not to come on this mission, but you're one stubborn SEAL."

"You're responsible for the death of my men? They trusted you. I fucking trusted you! Why would you do this?"

"They were the highest bidder. Bari realizes my worth." I hope Bari believes what I'm saying. "He knows my knowledge will make him more powerful and richer than any other person on this earth."

"Money! This is all about money for you!"

"It's always been about money."

I see the defeat in his face. "Let Drake go. Kill me, but let him go."

I kneel down in front of him. "I'd rather watch him die than kill you." Another truth from me. I run my hand down his uninjured side of his face. "I cared enough about you to try and get you out of this mission. Why couldn't you have obeyed orders?" I have to make this believable. "I'm going to miss fucking you. Better yet"—I stand— "maybe I'll keep you around and fuck you anytime I want."

Derrick's hands break free, and he grabs a grenade off the Bari's man's belt, pulling the pin. He topples over in the chair and covers Drake's body. I flee as quickly as I can. Bari runs close behind me, and I turn around, shoving him toward the grenade rolling on the floor.

CHAPTER 8

GENETICS

Two years later...

"Ms. Parrot, I have some DNA testing you need to look at right away. I sent it to your email," my assistant says, peeking his head through my door.

"I'll look at it when I get a minute." I finish signing a contract with my best dealer to get more results on organ procurement.

I disappeared for a year after Afghanistan. I changed my name and sold all my properties, including my ownership in the poppy fields, which alone made me millions to the next ruler of that area.

I'm finally where I want to be. Human trafficking is more profitable than what I ever imagined, especially now that we are selling organs to the highest bidders around the country. I should feel bad for the evil things I've done, but none of them measure up to how I felt about losing Derrick. I forced myself to move on and not look back.

"You really need to open the email." He steps further inside.

"What is the rush on this one?"

"We've found a match with your DNA."

I drop my pen, and my fingers fly over the keyboard to open the results in the email. I scan it. "Run it again to be sure," I bark.

"We've already run it three times. It's a ninety-eight percent match to yours. That's as good as it ever gets." He turns and walks out.

I've searched for my sister for years. I'd almost given up finding her. The only way that would ever happen is if she donated blood to the DNA bank in search of her identity. I look through her case file and then look her up on the internet. I buzz my assistant. "Buy me some time with this one, but I want her brought here. Do not harm her in any way. Do I make myself clear?"

"Yes, ma'am."

I can't believe I finally found her. I scan the pictures of her and any information I can find. She's pretty, but she has a sadness to her eyes. I touch her picture on the screen. Too bad she can never know about me, but I want to know her. What's her life been like? Is she in love? Does she have any children? A tinge of jealousy runs through me. I wish I could've escaped my upbringing. She has me to thank for that, but she'll never know that I saved her life.

I unlock the top drawer of my desk and take out the one and only thing I've kept from my childhood. The leather-bound journal is worn, but the pages are still intact. All my memories are stored safely inside it. Sometimes I look back at the little girl I wrote about and wish I could've saved her. Maybe I wouldn't be the monster I am today, and Derrick would've always loved me.

I type up a card for her and put it in the outgoing mail cart. It will give me some time to figure out how I want to handle things with her.

My assistant comes back into my office. "Do you want me to focus solely on your sister?"

"No. I want girls moving as usual. The auction is

booked. I have surgical procedures scheduled in our new facilities. Finding her changes nothing as far as production goes. I want her picked up next week and brought to our secure location. Notify me when we have her. When she does get here, no harm is to come to her unless I order it. I want our surgeon to see her to make sure she's okay. Don't indicate that to him. Let him think she's like everyone else around here."

One week later, I've received word that they have my sister in custody, so to speak. Tonight is an auction. I attend all of them, along with my second in charge. No one sees my face in the darkness, looking down on at them. I wear a mask over my face and eye patch, so there is no chance of anyone getting a good look at me. I've had multiple surgeries on my face, but my eye couldn't be saved.

When the lights go out and the girls are bound and marched on stage, I take my seat beside Karl. He's a face with no name to our employees, but they know he answers directly to me. My computer screen lights up, and the bidding begins. I glance out over the crowd, and my gaze locks on an old, familiar face. It can't be. How did he get out alive? I switch out of the bidding and search the names on our database. He's infiltrated our company under the name of Sam Larkin. *I remember you well, Theo Drake.* He can't be here after me, and he was too much of a good guy to be any part of this. I wonder? I search for the first time in a long time, Derrick Rebel. He's still a navy SEAL. He has an ugly scar down his face, but he's still as sexy as I recall.

I lean over to Karl. "That man sitting next to Lance, he's not one of us. You need to take care of him." My heart, which has been stone-cold since the last day I saw Derrick, races for the first time. "Find out what he's after and who."

He nods, and I get up before the auction has ended. I don't want there to be any mishaps where he might see me. I duck into my office, and that's where I spend the next several days, delving deeper into Theo and Derrick. I find their link and anger rages in me like never before.

* * *

It's another auction night, and I have no desire to be there, but I have to maintain my position. I pull on my mask and meet Karl at the door. We make our way to our seats when the lights go down. Within minutes, all hell breaks loose with gunfire being heard. I know in my gut that it's Theo and Derrick behind it. I rush to my office and take the gun from its magnet under my desk. Karl is right behind me. "Make sure you're armed. We're going to need it." I check our security monitor and see Derrick. "This is where we are going and the man that needs to be taken out.

We make our way down the stairs and into the room with rusted-out vats. "I know you're in here, Derrick," I say, with Karl walking behind me, sweeping the room with his gun. "I can make you a rich man."

"I don't want your dirty money!" his voice rings out.

I prowl toward him. "I don't have time to try to convince you to leave. You've never listened to me anyway, so you're forcing my hand. I don't want to kill you, but you're not leaving me any choice." I whisper to Karl to move the other direction and go behind him. "Come on, Derrick. I'm sure we can work this out. You can join forces with me. We were a good team at one point. I've missed us being together." That part is true. I've never met another man that could satisfy me like he could. I make calculated moves toward him.

Shots ring out. Karl is down, and Theo stands beside him, feeling for a pulse. Karl, all bloody, takes a swing at Theo, sending his gun flying. I keep inching closer to Derrick.

Karl and Theo fight, and Karl rips Theo's mechanical arm off. They struggle a few seconds longer before Theo regains his gun and fires. He gets up and falls back to the ground. Derrick comes out of his hiding place, rushing to Theo's side. I walk over to him and aim my gun.

I nudge Karl with my foot. "Too bad. I really liked him."

"Like you liked me?"

"That's where you're wrong, Derrick. I loved you. If you remember correctly, I tried to save you."

I squat down next to him but keep my gun steady. "Why do you have to play the hero?"

"Why'd you have to be such a lying bitch? You betrayed my team!" Spit flies from his mouth. "They're all dead because of you."

He's filled with hate after all these years. I don't want to focus on that. I still love him. "You wanted to marry me. We can still do that, you know. I've never forgotten the way you touched me." I stand.

"As a matter of fact, the night that I saw Theo sitting out there bidding on one of my girls, I knew you'd come, and I've thought about nothing else since." I lick my lips. "You can't tell me you don't miss us."

I show a moment of weakness, and his leg kicks out, knocking me to the ground. The gun fires as he rips it out of my hand, but it misses me. I look up, and he's standing over me with the gun.

"I fucking hate you!" he yells.

I slowly stand. "There's a fine line between love and hate, Derrick."

"There is no line for us. You killed anything I felt for you the day my men died."

I know he's lying when I see his hand shake. "I'm sorry about your men. If I could've had it play out any other way, I would've. I didn't come out of it unscathed. I lost my eye when you threw the grenade."

"Theo lost his arm, and I'm left with a nasty scar down my face. I could give a shit about your eye. Why did you do it? Was it all about money for you?"

"Yes, and the power it gave me."

"And this?" He waves his hand around.

"Do you know how much money I've made selling organs and trafficking women? I'm just one of many. You may stop me, but you're not going to stop this business. There's too much money to be made."

"How did you get so fucking evil?"

"I've always been this way. You were just too blind to see it. That's what made your team an easy target."

I see rage fill his features, and he aims the gun at my head. He's dripping in sweat, and he screams, "Ahhhh!" I know he wants to kill me. Maybe he should. Instead of pulling the trigger like I wish him to, he lowers the gun.

A woman's voice comes out of nowhere. "He can't kill you, but I can. My sister is dead because of you!"

I turn to face her and then look between the two of them. "She looks like me." I can't help but laugh. "I guess you're fooling yourself if you think you ever got over me."

"I'm nothing like you! You destroy people's lives for nothing more than greed." I watch her place both her hands on the gun.

"Don't do it," Derrick says, and she looks at him.

"Why, because you still love her?"

"No, because I want her to pay for what she's done. Rotting away in prison will be worse than death for her."

"She's smart. She'll find a way out."

She's right, I will. As her focus turns back to me, light floods the room, and a German swat team rushes inside. All three of us hit the ground. We're cuffed. Derrick shows his ID and tells his side of the story, and I'm hauled off to jail.

THORN'S REDEMPTION

Book 10

CHAPTER 1

REBEL

"Is she out of surgery yet?" Theo asks as he, Thorn, and Tate come crashing through the waiting room doors.

"The surgeon came out a few minutes ago and updated me. He said she'd lost a lot of blood, but they were able to repair the damage. They won't let me in to see her until she's in a room."

"That's good news," Theo says.

"Damn, she's one tough lady." Thorn adjusts his hat.

"She's alive, thanks to you." I shake Thorn's hand. "Any word on Nina's whereabouts?" I address my question to Tate because I know she's been working closely with Honor.

"No. But I did gather intel that Nina owns a port in Seattle. It appears to be how she's been moving her merchandise all this time. It's still been up and running even when she was in prison." She hands me a file, and I skim over it for anything that might look familiar.

"How did we miss this? It looks like she owned this before I met her."

"She used an alias and paid cash for it. We only found it because one of the guards at the prison overheard one of the men she paid off mention it, so we investigated deeper and made the connection." Tate points to a paragraph in the report.

"This has to be where she's headed and where our people are being held captive. Call Honor and tell her to have a plane ready in an hour. I'll meet you there. I want to see Fallon first."

"Why don't you stay here and let us handle it?" Thorn asks. "I'll take lead on the mission."

I debate internally. I want to go after Nina for what she's done, but I need to see Fallon, and my team is capable of going after her without me. "I should stay here until she's out of the woods." Knowing Fallon, she'll be pissed that I didn't go after Nina.

"We'll find her and our people." Theo puts his hand on my shoulder. "Hazel needs you here."

"Have Mad Dog and Lawson stay with Fiona and Honor. Once I know for sure that Fallon is okay, I'll bring Mad Dog with me. I want them moved to a secure location. Get ahold of Commander Lukas and make the arrangements." Theo gets on the phone as he and Tate head out the door. I stop Thorn by grabbing his shoulder. "Wait up a second." I don't talk until the other two are outside the hospital.

"I need you to be in charge. Theo and I've dealt with Nina for years. We need a different perspective on her. Who she really is, and how she operates."

"Yes, sir."

"When you get your hands on Nina, don't kill her. If anyone gets that pleasure, it will be me." I'm dead serious.

"I'm not making any promises. After what I watched her do to Fallon, I'm not taking any chances. She's a heartless bitch that won't hesitate to kill one of our own."

"We've got to get our people back first. If you kill her, they're as good as gone. Sean is tough and will fight her, and Lauryn is capable of outsmarting her, but I know nothing about your wife other than the fact that Nina said she's beautiful, and she'd make her a lot of money."

"Ex-wife, and yes, she is, and she'd never win against the likes of Nina."

"Nina said she has your wife and lover in the same room. Please tell me that you're not messing around with Lauryn."

"It's not what you think, but she and I knew one another in the past."

"We'll deal with this later. I need you to be focused."

"I am, sir."

"Get the hell out of here and find them." He rushes out the door the same time a nurse calls my name. "Derrick Rebel?"

"Yes." I walk over to her.

"Follow me, and I'll take you to Ms. Davis's room."

We walk through several doors then she badges into the double doors leading inside the ICU. She stops in front of glass doors, and I see Fallon. I don't wait; I rush into her room. Her eyes are closed, and she has oxygen tubing in her nose.

"Hey, doll." I lean down, kissing her forehead. Her eyes flutter a few times before they open.

"Rebel." Her voice is soft and sounds dry.

"I'm here. The doctor says you're going to be okay."

"Nina?"

"Don't worry about her. The Gunners are going after her and bringing back our family."

Her eyes close tight then open wide as she cringes when she tries to sit.

"Lay back down." I guide her shoulders toward the bed.

"Who did she take?"

"She has Lauryn, Thorn's ex-wife, and...Sean."

"Sean?" Her voice gets louder.

"He was at the bar at the time. It looks like he put up a good fight."

"Thorn has a wife?"

"Yeah, I don't know the details, but somehow she's connected with Lauryn. Thorn has a past with her that none of us were aware of."

"You have to go." She tries to get out of bed and holds her stomach.

"You're bleeding." I hold her side, trying to keep her from moving. "Nurse," I yell over my shoulder. "You've got to lay back down."

"You have to go after her. You're the only one that can stop her."

A nurse comes in and helps me get her back in bed. "It's too soon for you to be up. If I need to sedate you to keep you calm, I will," the nurse says, and I lift my hand so she can look at her. "You've ripped a couple of the stitches. I'll have to contact the doctor. Keep her still until I get back." She scurries from the room.

"I don't want to leave you." I sit on the edge of the bed next to her.

"You have to. If you don't, she'll never be out of our lives."

"I'll go only if you agree to follow doctor's orders. I'll station Mad Dog outside your room. I don't trust Nina to not come back here and finish what she started."

"I will, I promise, but don't let her get away. She'll destroy so many more people's lives, and you can't let that happen." Her eyes drift closed.

I'm so torn. I don't want to leave, but I know she's right. I'm the one she's really after, and I have to be the one to bring her down. My phone vibrates, and I tug it out of my pocket. It's my dad's number. "Damn it! With everything that's happened, I forgot about my parents flying in for the wedding." I step away from Fallon and answer it. I update him on what's happened but leave out the part about Sean. I don't want them to worry.

"I want you and Mom to get out of here. Go someplace you haven't been. Your lives may be in danger if you stay here or go back home. I'll call you when it's safe to return." I hang up and go back to Fallon's side.

"Our wedding," she whispers as her eyes continue to droop.

"It's okay, doll. We'll get married when all this is over." I watch her fall asleep then get on the phone with Mad Dog. I'm not leaving here until she's well guarded. I make arrangements for Honor to get me on a military plane. I don't want to hold up my team headed to Seattle. I then call Commander Lukas.

"I need more men as fast as you can get them to me. Four more in Portland and a backup team in Seattle." I tell him the new information about the port. "Honor and Lawson can brief them and get them up to speed. The team here needs to protect who's left behind. Mad Dog will be stationed outside Fallon's room." I hang up and wait impatiently for him to arrive.

"You're not to leave this post. Commander Lukas is sending backup. When they get here, Honor can direct one of them to the hospital to relieve you, until then, you don't move and you call me if anything happens."

"Yes, sir." He stands tall in the doorway.

I walk over to Fallon's bedside and lean down, kissing her lips. She doesn't budge from her sleep. "I love you, doll. I'll be back when Nina is either captured or dead, then we'll get married," I whisper.

I run to my truck and drive like a bat out of hell back to headquarters. Lawson and Fiona are held up in my office with Honor.

"This place isn't secure. As soon as back up comes, you two are going to a safe house." I point at Lawson and Fiona.

"We want to stay here and help." Lawson crosses his arms over his chest.

"Not going to happen. You can't help if you're dead," I bark.

"Nina didn't infiltrate this place. We're perfectly safe here, and I can help sweep the building." Lawson holds firm.

"I can help too," Fiona says, mimicking her father's stance.

"They are safer here where we can look out for each other. You said there was a team coming to headquarters," Honor adds.

"Not one of you is to leave this god damn building! Is that clear!" I slam my hands on the desk.

Lawson and Fiona nod. Honor says, "Yes, sir."

"Commander Lukas is sending four men. They'll rotate out with Mad Dog at the hospital. Two stand guard here at all times."

"I can take a shift too," Honor adds.

"Me, too," Lawson pipes in.

"Honor, I need your eyes on the computer, tracking information for us. You'll be our contact. Get satellite feeds from the Seattle port to our main system. Contact the nearest base and have them halt all movement on the water. Detain anyone in route, coming and going."

"Yes, sir." Her fingers fly over the keyboard. "Did Thorn and his team get off the ground yet?"

"They were air born ten minutes ago."

"Did you find a plane for me?"

"I did, sir, but all flights have been temporarily grounded. I was lucky to convince the pilot to get our men in the air."

"Why's that?"

"There's a big storm headed inland with winds that are unsafe for small airplanes."

"I don't give a shit about the weather. If you have

to, find me a private plane and a pilot that's willing to fly." My cell phone rings again.

"I'm disappointed. I wanted you to chase me," Nina says casually.

"Tell me where the fuck you are, and I'll gladly come after you." Is she still in Portland, or does she have men on the ground to know that I wasn't on the plane with my team?

"If I told you where I was, that would take all the fun out of the game."

"This is not a fucking game, Nina!" I yell into the phone.

"Why such the temper tantrum, Derrick? Did your girlfriend not make it?" she tisks.

I can keep Fallon safe if she thinks she's dead. "No," I say as solemnly as I can.

I hear a sharp intake of breath on the other end of the line. "You're lying." I swear I detect a sob in her voice. She doesn't give a shit about Fallon, and I know she's not sad for me.

"Wasn't that what you wanted, her dead?"

"Thorn should've been able to save her." This time her voice quivers.

"Is that guilt you're feeling for taking an innocent woman's life?"

"Of course not." Her tone harshens. "Why would I care if your precious girlfriend lives or dies?"

"You tell me? It wouldn't be like you to have a heart," I growl.

"My heart turned to stone a long time ago. I suggest if you don't want anyone else you care about to die that you play my game." She hangs up the phone, and I slam mine on the desk.

"What did you hear?" Honor asks. "Background noises?"

"Blades. Chopper blades in the distance."

Honor pulls up a map on her computer. "If she's still in Portland, these are the only two areas cleared for nonmedical choppers." She points to the screen. "If she's in Washington, the area is too broad for me to pinpoint."

"I'll go check these out while you find me a pilot and a plane. In the meantime, since Nina thinks Fallon is dead, make arrangements for Fallon to be brought here. She'll be safer amongst all of us, and our team won't have to be split. Someone will be assigned to guard her twenty-four seven." I turn to Lawson. "I want every inch of this place swept for bugs. Get it done before Fallon is released. Once she's here, I want Fiona barricaded in the room with her. I'm not risking losing one more person."

"I had to keep Fiona from not following after Theo. She feels like this is just as much her battle, if not more."

"That's the last thing that needs to happen. If you have to tie her down, then do it. You'll have your hands full with her and Fallon. I hope your wrestling skills are up to par." I chuckle.

CHAPTER 2

THORN

"The pilot says we are being rerouted due to the storm. He's going to maneuver us around it, and we'll have to land east of Seattle," Theo says as he sits in the seat next to me, latching himself into it.

"We can get a jeep when we land and trek to the port."

The airplane shifts, and it rattles us. "The storm that's coming must be a beast." Tate tightens her straps. "I hate airplanes."

Both Theo and I glance over at her. "How did you ever pass SEAL training if you hate to fly?"

"A lot of puking on my part, but I didn't let it win. Doesn't mean I have to like it."

"If you're going to throw up, please turn the other way." I point in the other direction.

"Damn it!" Theo groans.

"What is it?"

"I've lost signal with Honor. It has to be this damn storm." He pulls the mic out of this ear.

"We'll get in contact with her once we're on the ground."

"I wanted to make sure Fiona stayed put. She was tucking clothes and a gun in a backpack when I told her we were headed out."

"She's really come a long way in a short period of time."

"She has, and I'm so damn proud of her, but she's a little too feisty at times."

"Nothing wrong with a gutsy woman." I laugh.

"No, but I like my balls where they are, perfectly intact." He chuckles and looks at his crotch.

"Other than her fiery spirit, how are the two of you doing?"

He runs his hand over his head. "I didn't think I'd ever love someone as much as I do her. I know it sounds like I'm being a wuss, but I'd give her the world if she wanted it."

"Naw, man. Sounds like you found your heart."

"What about you?"

"What about me?"

"His heart belongs to the military," Tate snorts. "There's no room for a woman in it."

"That can't be true. According to Nina, there's an ex Mrs. Beckham."

"That was a long time ago, and a period of my life I'd like to forget."

"You must've loved her at one time to marry her."

"I thought I did, but I chose this life, and it ruined our marriage. Tate's right. I love the military more."

"But why have you hidden the fact that you were married?"

"Why don't you mind your own damn business?"

"Because we're brothers, and we help each other and have each other's backs."

"I don't need my back covered on this."

"What about Dr. Ruth?" Tate raises her brows. "What does she have to do with your wife?"

"You two need to back off and focus on the mission and leave my private life out of it." I grit my teeth in anger. I don't want to expose mine and Lauryn's affair. It was a long time ago, and she's made it clear that nothing will happen between us again, even though I know her body came to life the moment she saw me. I was an inexperienced young lover when we were together. I'd love to have her wrapped in my arms to show her the man I am now.

They're both quiet for a second. "I shot and killed my father," Theo breaks the silence. "I'm not proud of it, but it changed my life."

"Why are you telling me this?" I yank my bandanna off my head.

"I thought if I shared something personal with you, that maybe you'd be more willing to open up."

"This is not the Dr. Phil show, and not everyone has to wear their heart on their sleeve." I'm gruff in my delivery, but I want him to stop.

"And, not everyone has to be an asshole either. You joined our team, and no one really knows you." Tate puts her two cents in with Theo.

"I'm not here to be warm and fuzzy with you. I'm focused on the job."

"Maybe that's why your marriage didn't last long," Tate scoffs.

I unbuckle and forge out of my seat. "My marriage didn't last because my wife fucked another man!" I storm toward the pilots and stumble when the plane dips from an air pocket. I steady myself with my hand on the ceiling. Damn it, why did I let them get to me? I'm a goddamn SEAL, and I let these two force a conversation that I don't want to relive.

I open the cockpit door. "How long before we land?"

"We have to keep moving further east. This storm is dangerous. I'm estimating another hour," the pilot says. "You may want to stay buckled in. We're going to hit some pretty high winds."

I stomp back out, but instead of sitting between them, I strap in the seat across from them. "We're hitting high turbulence. The pilot says it will be another hour. How about instead of delving into my past, we look over the schematics of the Seattle port."

Tate takes out her laptop.

"I'm sorry she cheated on you, brother. No one deserves that kind of dishonesty in a relationship." Theo looks sincere.

"I can't connect in this weather. As soon as we land, I'll pull it up, and we can look over it on the drive to Seattle." Tate stuffs her computer back in her bag.

"What about you, Tate? You ever been in love?" Theo looks at her.

"Oh, no, we are not making this about me," she snorts.

"I think the woman protests a little too much." Theo laughs.

"Leave her alone," I say gruffly. I like Theo. He's a damn good SEAL, but I'm in no mood for touchy-feely shit.

"I'm just trying to have a conversation to kill time."

"You want to converse, let's come up with a plan to get our people back alive. Nina has proven to be ruthless and very resourceful, and on top of it all, she already has a head start. She's done her homework and knows something personal about each of us. She has the advantage of knowing our Achilles' heel. I say we use the time to figure out what hers is, what's her weakness?"

"Captain Rebel," Tate responds.

"He may be a small thread of weakness for her, but there has to be something else," Theo says.

"I agree. What do we know about her past? Where she grew up? Does she have any family?"

"Rebel couldn't find anything on her past. It's like she never existed," Theo responds.

"Everyone has a past. We just haven't dug deep enough. She knows us. We need to find out what drives her, or we'll never stop her."

"What makes you think it's more than Captain

Rebel? I know women will do crazy things for the men they love, including killing whoever is in their way," Tate says.

"He was a pawn in her game, and he disturbed her ultimate goal. I think in her sick mind, she cared about him as much as a woman like her is capable of loving another person. But she disappeared for years with no contact with him until we infiltrated her company. It pissed her off," Theo adds.

"Here is the question." I tap my finger to my temple. "What made her so cold-hearted? Something in her past created the woman she is today. That's what we need to find out in order to play her game, and it's up to us to figure it out before it's too late. Rebel's too close to the situation." I tie my bandanna back on my head.

"He's right. I'll get Honor to do some digging as soon as we're back in commission on the radios." Tate presses her earpiece.

"Do you really believe that Nina has our people held up in the port?" Theo crosses his arms.

"She's the type of woman that's going to leave us scraps unless we catch her off guard. My bet is on one or two of them being held there, but Sean will be the last person we'll find. He's the closest to Rebel, and he'll be the final hand she shows."

"The three of us can't fight her. We'll need more men," Tate responds.

"Agreed, but we are all we got when we hit the ground. Rebel is having a team sent to meet us at the port. They'll be our support, but we better have a damn good strategy in mind by the time we get there. With the information we have on her, I'm sure she already knows where we're landing, and she's one step ahead of us. We have to make her misstep before we catch her. She's owned this building for a long time. There has to be something there to give us a clue. A piece of her is there in that building, and we have to find it and use it against her."

"Do you really think she's stuck around?" Tate asks.

"My gut says yes. She wants to watch us play her game of cat and mouse."

"The one thing I do know about Nina is that there has to be some financial gain in it for her. She's always been about the highest bidder," Theo remarks.

"This time is different. It's personal. Rebel took her down, and she lost a lot of money. I think it was pennies to her, but he keeps getting in her way. She could have disappeared once she broke free. Instead, she came after all of us."

"Rebel won't hesitate in killing her this time," Theo adds. "Not after what she did to Fallon."

"She's cold-blooded. I should've stopped her when I had the chance."

"You made the right choice in saving Fallon," Tate says. "We'll get Nina, and she'll pay for her crimes."

"Not if she's dead," I say sternly and none of them argue the point.

The plane jars us again, and Tate looks green. "Where are you from, Tate?" I try to distract her.

"Mister, I don't want to tell anything personal wants to know something about me?" she chimes in, and Theo chuckles.

"She's got a point." He grins.

I press my lips together. "Dr. Ruth was one of the base counselors where I was stationed. She was just starting her career, and she was assigned to me. She tried to save a marriage that was unsalvageable. So, yes, I knew her."

"You knew her, so what?"

I glance at Tate, and she has a look of understanding in her eyes. Theo remains clueless.

"You knew her." Tate smiles.

"What am I missing?" Theo asks.

"Nothing other than our lives have collided

again." I shrug him off. Funny how our lives can be fated together. I never thought I'd see her again, but here I am, now trying to save her life that's in danger because of our past. One small link in time may change her life forever.

CHAPTER 3

NINA

"Zoom in on their faces." I point to the room where Maxim has his camera closed in on the women. He's been a loyal employee for years. I met him not long after my affair with Derrick. He's a plaything with a brilliant technical mind. Not so great in bed, but a bad lay is better than no sex. No man will ever compare to the heights Derrick could take my body. He made me want more and feel more than I ever thought possible. "If you have to kill one of them, make sure it's the smart one, not the one worth a million dollars simply because she's got a pretty face."

"I think the other one is gorgeous." He smiles.

"She's pretty but too smart for her own good."

"I like brains on a woman." His gaze scans over me. "A hot body doesn't hurt either."

"You'll save the one I can sell," I snip. I'm in no mood for him, especially since I've been around Derrick. That man always makes my skin heat up in more ways than one.

He flips over to another screen. "He's on the move."

"Where are you headed, Derrick?" I say, leaning close to the monitor. "Has his team landed yet?"

"No word on them yet. They've more than likely been diverted to another airport outside of Seattle because of the storm."

"Phone the men and tell them to be ready at the port. They'll need to move quickly. I need to make a phone call." I walk around the old metal corrugated building that's been closed for years. Only a few blocks from where Derrick calls headquarters, it was a great find. I've been able to plant a few bugs and keep an eye on the comings and goings of his team. This timber factory was booming in its day. Left behind are empty rooms that housed engineering offices, old rusted equipment, tools, industrial shelving, and a faded company emblem on the wall. The smells of wood and stains still hang in the crevices. I walk out back to a large delivery bay area and sit on the concrete floor, dangling my legs over the side, and find the number I want.

"Fallon Davis's room."

"I'm sorry, but there's no one admitted under that name," the voice on the other end says.

"Look again. Try Fallon Rebel." Surely he didn't marry her.

"Nothing under that name, either."

I push the button to end the conversation. "I guess there's only one way to find out." I call Maxim's number. "I want you to pull up the cameras at headquarters and tell me who is in the building." I wait.

"The cameras aren't operational. They must've found them."

"Damn it." I hang up and dial Derrick.

"Where are you headed, lover? Didn't anyone tell you there was a storm coming?" I hear his growl.

"When I find you, I'm going to kill you, Nina."

"Being that I know where you are, it seems that I have the upper hand."

"Don't get too comfortable. That can and will change at any moment."

"Sean's a sweetheart, by the way. He's very charming and has the all-American boy looks. Too bad he had to put up such a fight. He'll have a nasty scar to match yours."

"This is all part of your game to bait me, isn't it?" His tone is terse. "Why don't you tell me what it is you really want and let my team go?"

"I wanted to not get caught and lose time in prison. You cost me loads of money."

"That's what it always comes back to for you. You still have plenty of money that wasn't found, so why don't you let it go?"

"Let it go?" I tap my finger to my lips. "Have you ever been hungry enough to eat out of garbage bins? Or, if you wanted clothes you had to steal them from a laundry mat? Better yet, give up someone because you knew their life would be better if they weren't trapped in a world of disgust or a life without love in it?"

"Is that where your hate stems from, your childhood? I'm sorry for the things that happened to you as a kid, but you're an adult now. You don't have to be stuck in the past."

"You're right. I don't, and I'll never be put in a vile situation again. I choose to be filthy rich and never want or need for anything."

"At all cost to other people's lives."

"Yes."

"I feel sorry for you. You're the true definition of a narcissist."

"No. I don't want your pity. That's one thing I've always loved about you, Derrick. You don't pity people. You take what life has thrown at them, and you make them stronger, so don't go giving me your fucking sympathy."

"What do you know about love, Nina? You have to give love to get it back."

"You loved me even when I felt nothing more than a small amount of emotion toward you. And, you have no idea what I've done for love. I wouldn't have..." I stop myself from telling him about my sister.

"You wouldn't have what, Nina?"

"You need to stop worrying about me and concentrate on how to save your people, or they're going to end up just like your Gunner team. They've already been ambushed. Now it's time for the slaughter." I hang up when he starts yelling.

I get up and go back into the room with Maxim. "Pack up this equipment. We're moving locations. As soon as this storm lets up, get a boat ready."

"Where are we going?"

"We're going to hell, Maxim. Get Derrick's brother out of the freezer, that's if he's still alive by now. He's going with us." I take one of his guns from his holster.

"You going somewhere?"

"I need to see something for myself. Be ready to leave when I get back."

I storm out to my rental van and head straight for the hospital. I toss the gun in my purse and slide in a back door when an employee comes out for a smoke break. I walk down a long hallway past a locker room. I slip inside and take a white coat out of a locker. I tuck my hand in the pocket to find a hospital ID. "Lucky girl." I find it easy to blend in when you act like you belong. I stop at a nurse's station.

"I need to find out what room my patient was sent to after surgery." I flash the secretary my badge with my thumb over the picture. She barely looks up.

"What's your patient's name?"

"Fallon Davis."

"It says here, she's deceased."

"Just tell me what room she went to?" Derrick could easily have it added to her file with his connections.

"It looks like after she transferred out of ICU, she was put in a private room. Room number 305."

I nod and head to the elevators, but change my mind and take the stairs. When I reach the third floor, I crack the door open and look down the long hallway. I see one of Derrick's men outside a room. "You lying bastard. You'll pay for that." I step back into the stairwell and call Maxim. "Temporary change of plans. I need one of our doctors on staff to give me a sedative. We've got a patient that needs to come with us on our trip. You might want to tell him it's got to be big enough to take down a horse." Derrick's man is the size of a stallion. "Tell him to have it delivered to a coffee shop directly across the street from the hospital. I'll be waiting for him."

"Yes, ma'am." Maxim always does what I ask without question. The next call I make is to the head of operations at the port.

"I need you to shut down the port immediately. Code red is in place." I hang up, knowing he understands. He'll have the shipment of women gone, along with all their records. We've kept the bare minimum around, so in case of an emergency, it could be cleaned out within an hour. He'll either put the crate of women on a boat, or he'll have them moved to another location. My desk will be his second priority. He doesn't know where my safe is located, and neither does anyone else, so it will be secure.

I sip on a cup of coffee until I see the familiar

face of the doctor who's always been more than willing to give me what I need for a handsome price. I've made him tons of money, and I know where he's hidden the bodies of his enemies. He's more than happy to help for a price.

He sits at the table next to mine. He bends down like he's tying his shoe and puts a syringe in my open bag. "This should do the trick," he whispers, then leaves.

While I finish my coffee, I call Maxim again. "I need you here to help me. My van is parked out back. I'll prop open the hospital door directly across from the van so you can get inside. Take the stairwell to the third floor and wait for me. Make sure Sean is not able to move before you leave. We'll come back and get him."

"I'll be there in fifteen minutes."

I throw my empty cup in the trash on the way out. I move the van closer to the door and press the button to lock it. I wave my badge in front of the scanner by the door, and it opens. I dig a paperclip out of my purse and bend it, shoving it in the hole so that the door won't fully close. I make my way back up the stairs and peek out. Derrick's man hasn't moved. A few minutes later, I hear heavy footsteps coming up the stairwell, and I know it's Maxim.

"There's a large man guarding the door. I need to get in that room." I pull the syringe out of my purse, handing it to him and securing the gun in my hand. "He knows my face, and I can't let him see me. I'll keep my head down and walk in behind you. Jab this in his neck and shove him in the room. I'll take it from there."

He nods.

Walking out in front of me, I stay closely hidden behind him. When he walks past Mad Dog, I let him see my face. He goes for his gun, and Maxim thrusts the needle into this neck and quickly moves him inside the room. He lowers him to the floor before he can fall with a loud thud. I step further inside and see Fallon, and she happens to have a visitor, Fiona.

I grasp my gun firmly. "Two for the price of one." I snatch Fiona by the hair. "If you so much as make a peep, I'll kill her." I jerk her head back, and Fallon sits up.

"What do you want?" Fallon asks, raising her hands.

"You're going to come with me."

"I'll cooperate if you leave her alone."

"You'll do as I say, not the other way around." I laugh at her audacity, thinking she's going to tell me what to do.

"I'd rather us both die than you take her. It's your choice. If you want me alive, you'll let her go."

"Fine. She's caused me enough trouble anyway." I don't want to deal with the likes of this wild cat.

"Don't do it, Fallon. My dad is on his way up. He'll stop her."

I turn her in my arms and hit her in the face with my gun. Maxim catches her before she falls to the ground. I direct my aim at Fallon. "Get up. Now!"

She slowly climbs out of bed and walks over to me. "Rebel will find me."

"That's the plan. You're going to walk down the hallway and follow him to the stairwell." I indicate Maxim with my head. "Don't think about yelling out or trying to escape. I'll have this gun aimed at your back the entire time."

Maxim opens the door and leads the way. Fallon, to my surprise, fully cooperates. She follows him down the stairs without one word. I unlock the van door, and she gets in the back. I climb in with her and Maxim drives.

"I'll die before I let you hurt Rebel," she cries.

"How sweet. I don't want you to die."

"You have a funny way of showing it when you shot me."

"If I wanted you dead"—I press the gun to her

chest—"I would've shot you in the heart, not the stomach. As far as Derrick goes, in the end, he'll choose me over you."

"He hates you."

"Hate is such a strong word. When he hears what I have to offer him, you'll be a ghost in the wind to him."

"You're sicker than I thought," she says.

"Maybe so, but I'll have him, not you. You've had everything good in life, but you'll not get the only man I've really ever cared about."

CHAPTER 4

REBEL

"Lawson, can you hear me? You're breaking up. I'm getting about every third word."

"Did...her...storm...Fallon."

"What about Fallon?" I screech the truck around in the opposite direction. "I don't know if you can hear me or not, but I checked out both the chopper locations. Nina is not at either one of them, and she wasn't on their manifest."

"Fiona...hospital."

"Shit!" I hang up and call Honor. "Hey, is Lawson with you?"

"No, sir...I."

"He called me, but our connection was hit or miss, and I couldn't understand him."

"Sir, you need to get to the hospital right away."

"Has something happened to Fallon?"

"I...she..."

"Spit it out!"

"Nina took her."

I slam on the brakes, and I jerk forward, hitting my forehead on the steering wheel. "What did you say?"

"Someone was with her, and he drugged Mad Dog. Lawson had taken Fiona over for a visit. She was stir crazy, and he thought it would do both the girls some good. Nina struck Fiona in the face with her gun."

I press the gas pedal all the way to the floor. "Fucking A! How does this happen.? We have a navy SEAL planted at her door, and she kidnaps Fallon!"

"They drugged him, sir."

"I'll be there in five minutes. Tell Lawson to stay put. How is Fiona?"

"Banged up, but she'll be okay."

"Call Commander Lukas and order a lockdown on the city."

"Already done, sir."

"I want military at every small airport in a hundred-mile radius of Portland. She won't get on a major airline. No planes in the air. Do you understand me?"

"Yes, sir. I'm contacting all the ports to have them shut down too."

"It's harder to stop the waterways but the air we can control. Also, put the local police on the Vancouver bridge. Get her picture out to all the major broadcasts. Nobody crosses over into Washington from Portland."

"I'm on it, sir."

"Has the extra team arrived yet?"

"They are walking in the door as we speak."

"Have them stay put. As soon as I'm done at the hospital, I'll be there to brief them. Have the war room ready. Every picture you can find of our team and Nina needs to be plastered all over the board. I want every bit of information you have on Nina. Bank accounts, properties she owns, where she grew up, everything. You'll have to dig deep and be creative to outsmart her."

"Yes, sir."

I pull up front at the hospital and leave the truck running. I'm in full military garb, so no one stops me. I toss the valet my keys. "Keep it running," I bark and make it to the elevator doors as they open. I ride it up to the ICU to learn she had been moved to another room. I hike down the stairs and burst through the door of room number 305. Mad Dog is coming to in the bed, and Lawson is standing over Fiona, holding an ice bag to her cheek.

"What the fuck happened?"

"I brought..." Lawson starts.

"Not you, him." I point to Mad Dog.

"A man larger than me walked by. I was keeping an eye on him, and the next thing I know, Nina was behind him. I went for my gun, but he stabbed me in the neck with a needle." He rubs the spot on his neck. "That's the last thing I remember, sir."

I press the heel of my hands to my forehead. "And, I told you not to leave headquarters!" I all but shout at Lawson.

"It's my fault. I was stir crazy and wanted to check on Fallon." Fiona sniffs. "She saved me."

"What do you mean?"

"She convinced Nina not to take me with her. She said she'd die before she'd let me go. She told Nina she'd cooperate if she'd leave me behind."

I take a deep, calming breath. "Are you okay?"

She shakes her head.

"I want all of you in my truck right now!" I bark, and they all move. Mad Dog is a little off-kilter, so I lead him by the arm. He jerks it away.

"I can manage." I know he's pissed about what happened, and knowing him, he wants his revenge.

I speed through traffic, back to headquarters. "I want all of you in the war room so I can keep an eye on you." I lead them through the door, straight to the room where everyone is gathered.

"I don't have time for formal introductions. Have you found out any new information on Nina?" I direct my question at Honor.

"She owns the old lumber facility a few blocks down." She projects her findings on the big screen.

"That's how she's been able to see our every move. You two, go sweep her building." Two soldiers get up and leave.

"I found her cameras and disabled them," Lawson says.

"How did she get them installed?"

"It must have been when our system went down, and a crew was sent over to repair it," Honor adds.

"Find the team that repaired it. Have Commander Lukas question them."

I place my hands on the table and lean. "What are your names?" I ask the two soldiers that are left.

"Seaman Remington Michaels."

"Seaman Van Williams."

"Remington, you're with me." I turn to Mad

Dog. "You and Williams will stay here and be back up. Nobody leaves this time. You got it?" I point to Lawson.

"Yes, sir."

"Honor, did you get satellites up and running?"

"They're running but not much visibility with the storm."

"I'm sick to death of this goddamn storm!" I slam my fists on the table. "The stakes just got higher with Nina taking Fallon as her prisoner. We have no time to waste. I want a plan ready to go by the time I get to the airport. Not excuses."

I march to the weapons room with Mad Dog and Remington behind me. Mad Dog fills my duffel bag with weapons and ammo. "Are you sure I can't go with you, sir? I have a score to settle with that bitch."

"Take a number. I know how devious she is and how determined she is when she wants something."

"I'm sorry, Captain. This is all my fault."

"Actually, it's all mine, but that's about to end. I'm going to play her game, but I'm going to do it smarter than her." I pick up a gun. "And with force."

Mad Dog fills a bag with equally as much firepower for Remington. He flings it over his shoulder, and we stop at Honor's desk before heading out.

"Did you get a plane?"

"Yes, sir. It will be fueled and ready to go. I already texted you the address."

"Get that satellite as clear as you can, and don't take your ears off. Keep your eyes peeled and let me know what you see."

"Our men are pulling up to the port." She points to one of the screens.

"Good, I'm on my way. Lock this place down behind me," I order, and Remington follows me out.

I get behind the wheel and drive as fast as I can. The sky is dark and looming, and the wind has picked up. "How long have you been a SEAL?" I might as well get to know the man who is going to have my six.

"Five years, sir."

"What's your specialty?"

"Explosives."

"Setting them or disarming them?"

"Both, sir."

"I have a feeling before all is said and done, we'll be utilizing your skill set."

"Whatever you need, sir."

"What I need is to stop this woman once and for all."

CHAPTER 5

THORN

We parked a mile from the port and trekked toward it. The wind is blowing the rain horizontally, and it's pouring down so hard it's obscuring our vision, along with it getting dark outside.

"Honor, can you hear me?" I try the mic.

I get a lot of static before she comes in somewhat clear. "Men have arrived for backup. They're held up west of the building near a container labeled forty-three. Do you copy?"

"Roger, that."

"With the storm, I can't get a visual."

"We're going in blind," I turn to tell Theo and Tate. "Let's get to the west side of the port to meet our backup." We change directions and locate container forty-three. One man is on lookout and raises his weapon when he sees us heading toward him. "Stand down. Seaman Thorn Beckham with the Gunner team." I raise a hand in the air.

"Dagger with Delta Force," he responds.

"Commander Lukas sent in the big guns," Tate says.

"How many men do you have?"

"There's twelve of us. I was instructed to wait for you, then sweep the building. Now that you're here, we'll take over the mission. Fall in step with my men." He opens the container door, and eleven soldiers stand. He points and starts giving out orders. "You two, east side of the building. You and you, west side. You four cover the front, and you three with me in the back." He turns to us. "One of you a sniper?"

"I am." Theo steps forward.

"Take her and get on the roof," he tells him.

"Beckham, I want you to lead my men in the front of the building." His men nod in understanding. "The goal is to capture, not kill anyone unless absolutely necessary."

Each team member scatters with weapons ready.

The wind is blowing so hard that the metal building creeks sounding like the roof is being ripped off. We make our way to the front and wait for the all-clear.

"Everyone in place?" Dagger is on the radio.

"Yes, sir," each team member answers, including Theo.

"Sweep the building and meet in the middle."

A shot rings out as one of the soldiers shoots off the doorknob. The building is stormed in from all sides with lights from weapons peering through it.

"It's empty," Dagger says. "Check the upstairs offices and you men"—he points—"I want every container opened and searched."

"Tate, get down here," I say over my mic. "She's our forensic expert. If they left a trace behind, she'll find it," I tell him.

"Leave the sniper on the roof in case someone shows up," he orders.

"Theo, stay where you are. Radio me if you see any signs of movement other than us."

"Roger."

"No signs of anyone!" one of his men yells from the top platform of the stairs.

Tate is soaking wet when she walks into the building.

"I need you to find any clue that was left behind." She nods and starts searching right away.

"It doesn't look like you'll need us here unless we find anyone in the containers." Dagger steps up to me.

"Maybe not here, but stay close by in case we find something."

Once a thorough search is done, he leads his men out.

"Where's everyone going?" Theo's voice is in my ear.

"We didn't find anything. They'll be on standby. Get your ass down here."

A few minutes later, he's inside the building, dripping water on the floor. He takes his hat off and shakes his head. "It's raining like a son of a bitch."

"We'll make camp here for the night."

"I found a hidden safe," Tate yells down from one of the rooms upstairs.

We both take off in her direction.

"It looks like an air vent." She points, and we walk into an office. There's an expensive-looking desk sitting in the middle of the room, totally out of place from the decor.

"This has Nina written all over it." Theo drags his hand on the top of it.

“Search every inch of it.” I walk over to the vent. “How did you know it was here?” I ask Tate.

“By tapping on the wall.” She wraps her knuckles in a few places, and when she gets closer to the vent, the sound dulls. “A vent doesn’t change the sound behind it.”

“Have you tried to open it?”

“I could only remove the vent. I’m not tall enough to reach it.”

I pull a small flashlight out of my gear and aim it at the keypad. I try the numbers that look warn. “It could be any combination of things.” I activate my earpiece again. “Honor, you still there?” Nothing but static answers me. “Captain Rebel.” More static.

“We could blow it up,” Theo says from behind us.

“It might damage whatever’s inside,” Tate responds.

“Anything in the desk?”

“No, not even fingerprints. It’s all been wiped clean.”

“Chances are, whatever was inside the safe is gone too,” Tate adds.

“Maybe, but we have to get inside it. Theo, any of the numbers mean anything to you? Zero, two, seven.”

"It's usually four numbers to open a safe." Tate stands on her tiptoes to look.

"Try doubling one of the numbers," Theo joins us.

"Zero, zero, two, seven. Zero, two, two, seven. Zero, two, seven, seven."

"Wait, the first one. Change the numbers around, and you have Rebel's birthday."

Tate and I look at one another.

"Zero, seven, two, zero." He flashes his light at the numbers.

"It can't be that easy." Tate laughs.

I reach up and push the numbers in order that Theo blurted out, and the safe opens. "I'll be damned," I say in disbelief.

"Maybe we all have it wrong, and this is about our fearless leader," Tate says as I reach up and pull the contents out and lay it on the desk.

"It's an old journal." Tate picks it up.

"And two birth certificates. One has Nina's name on it, the other one says baby girl. Parent's names are scratched out on both of them."

"Nina was born in Forks, Washington. That's roughly four hours northwest of Seattle."

"This has to be a trap. Why would she leave this

behind." Tate flips through a couple of pages in the journal.

"She didn't think it would be found. There has to be a link in this journal. Something that will give us the edge over her." The roof sounds like it's being lifted by the wind as I speak.

"We need to get out of here," I say. Tate tucks the journal and the other papers in her backpack. "Let's make it back to the jeep and find a place out of this storm."

We take off in a run to the jeep and head north of town. The streets are dead and stoplights are out, swaying by their lines. There's a small hotel with flickering lights in the window. An old mom-and-pop style place. "Stay here. I'll get us a room."

"Two!" Tate yells.

Because of the storm, reservations had been canceled, and I'm able to get three rooms. The couple was sweet and gave me all of them for free. Their son was retired military, and they like to help out whenever they can.

I wave Theo and Tate in from the jeep and toss them each a set of keys. "Get some sleep. I'll try to get Rebel on the radio."

"I'm not tired. I'm going to stay up and see what I can learn from Nina's journal," Tate says.

We depart ways, and my first stop is a hot shower. When I come out, Theo is sitting on the end of my bed. "How did you get in my room?"

"The old credit card in the door trick." He chuckles.

"Why are you in my room?" I throw on a pair of sweatpants.

"I was able to reach Fiona on the hotel line. Nina kidnapped Fallon."

"What the fuck? Rebel was having her guarded."

"One of Nina's men drugged Mad Dog. She said Fallon saved her."

"I bet Rebel is beside himself."

"He was headed out with a new team member. She said Honor arranged a plane for him, but I doubt he's getting off the ground in this weather."

"I don't know, with Fallon missing, he's bound to accomplish anything to get her back." I connect my earpiece. "Captain, you got your ears on?"

"...hard...winds too...emergency..." static.

"Shit." I reach over and grab the landline. There's a dial tone for a split second before it goes dead along with the lights. Theo's flashlight clicks on. "There's nothing we can do but sit and wait. I'll keep trying to get Honor, but until this storm dies down, I don't think we'll be in contact with any of them."

Tate slings the door open. "You two okay in here?"

"Do any of you know how to knock?"

She ignores me and sits beside Theo and shines his light on the journal. "The other birth certificate belonged to Nina's sister."

"Did you find a name?" Theo asks.

"According to what she wrote, her parents never bothered to name the baby. Nina called her Rella."

"Damn. That's cold," I say.

"There's more." Tate swallows hard. "Nina gave the baby away. She was digging in a dumpster to get something to eat, outside a fire station. She had laid the baby down on the ground when she got in the dumpster. Nina hid when a fireman came out the door. He saw the baby and picked her up. Nina didn't stop him. She never saw her sister again."

"No wonder she's so screwed up." Theo jerks the book from her hand. "If she's from Forks, we should be able to find this firehouse. Maybe someone will remember the baby."

"It's worth a shot. I'll head that way in the morning after I've connected with either Honor or Rebel."

They both get off the bed and walk over to the door. Theo stops and turns around, smiling. "You knew her." He looks like he discovered a secret.

"Knew who?" I ask.

"Dr. Ruth. Now I get it." He grins.

Tate tugs him out by the ear. "Come on, lover boy. Leave him alone before he kills you in your sleep."

CHAPTER 6

REBEL

The pilot made an emergency landing on an empty strip of highway on the coast of Oregon. He routed us west to try to fly around the back end of the storm, but the winds shifted, forcing us to land. I attempt to reach Thorn as soon as we're outside the plane.

"Thorn, do you copy?" Nothing. "Beckham." Silence.

"We need to keep moving, sir." Remington holds his hat down to keep the rain from dripping on his face.

We head toward the downtown area of Astoria. Every building is dark, and the small-town streets are empty.

"In here." Remington shoulders open the door to

a movie theater. The pilot follows him inside, and I do the same. The power flickers on, and the entryway lights up. Movie posters and life-size cardboard characters line the walls.

"The final Avengers movie." Remington stands beside the life-size cut out of Ironman. "I've been wanting to see this movie."

"If you can run a projector, now's your chance. It looks like we'll be here until the storm has blown over."

"My uncle owned a theater about the size of this place back home in Florida." He hops over the half door to the concession stand. "I even know how to make popcorn." He turns on the machine.

I walk around the theater, continuing to try to reach any of my team members. I only hope that Thorn found something at the port that will lead us to Fallon. I know she's tough, but she's injured, and she has to be frightened. Maybe she took her to wherever she's keeping Sean. He'd die to keep her safe. I push open the doors to the seating area of the movie and sit in the back row. A few minutes later, the movie screen lights up. The pilot and Remington join me with their hands full of popcorn and drinks. They sit in the row in front of me.

"Do you want some popcorn?" Remington asks.

"No. I'm good, but I'll take a drink."

He hands me a soda. With Fallon gone, I can't stomach the thought of food. I raise my leg and pull off my walking boot. My foot aches and is swollen from running on it. It hasn't fully healed from being broken.

I close my eyes for a brief moment, picturing Fallon here with me. She loves a good action film as much as the guys do. I'd give anything for her to be here safe with me. When this is all over with, and Nina is dead, I'm marrying her and taking her away on a real honeymoon. She deserves it for all she's been through. Honestly, I'm not sure why's she stuck around. Her life has been nothing but chaos since we met. I'm lucky she loves me. Maybe I'll give up being a SEAL and settle down into a normal life. It'd be nice to have a few rug rats running around. Let's just hope they look like her and not my ugly mug. I run my hand down the deep scar on my face, and then I remember Nina's words about Sean. I've brought him nothing but trouble too. He's a good man and the best brother I could've ever asked for. I have to find him before it's too late.

I can't just sit here and watch a movie while god knows what's happening to my family and the others. I put my boot back on and high tail it out of the theater.

"Honor! Damn it, answer me!" I growl.

"I can barely hear you, but I'm here, sir."

"We had to land. The storm was too rough. We're in Astoria. As soon as the weather clears, we'll get back in the air."

"Sir, I got a satellite visual with confirmation of Nina and three others chartering a yacht on the coast in Cannon Beach. They're anchored out waiting for the storm to slow down."

"Damn, that's not far from here. Send me their location. We'll head out now. Any word from Thorn?"

"Theo called Fiona. The port was empty, but they found a journal that belongs to Nina. Tate is digging into it."

"If they reach out again, tell them to do whatever it takes to get our people back. Follow where Nina takes them."

"Will do, sir."

"How are things there?"

"We're holding down the fort, so to speak. Lawson and Fiona are tucked away. Mad Dog refuses to sleep. He's beating himself up over Fallon. Williams is trying to calm him down."

"I'll talk to him when I get back. Keep me posted on the satellite feed and if the yacht takes out to deeper water." I disconnect. At least I know Fallon is alive and not too far out of reach. I run back into the movie. "Get your gear. We're moving," I bark at Remington.

"What about the storm? We can't get back in the air." He shoves a handful of popcorn in his mouth as he climbs over the seat.

"We'll be on foot. No need for you to follow," I tell the pilot.

I open the theater door to a gust of wind and rain. "We need to head south."

"Screw this." Remington runs by me to an old pickup truck deserted in the parking lot. He yanks the door hard, and it opens. He gets inside and kneels down under the steering wheel, and a few seconds later the engine sputters to life. "Get in!" he yells over the sound of the pounding rain. He hops behind the wheel, and I climb in the passenger side, throwing my bag in the middle along with his.

"I hope this piece of crap runs."

"I've never met an engine that didn't like me." He chuckles and forces it into gear. "I can take any motor apart and put it back together blindfolded.

That's why I'm so good with explosives. Same principle. You just have to know what drives them."

"Turn left here. Head to Cannon Beach."

The rain is coming down so hard the wipers can't keep up. We're moving, but it's at a snail's pace.

"So, the woman that Nina kidnapped, she's your girlfriend?" he asks while focusing on the road.

"Fiance."

"I had one of those once. She couldn't handle a SEAL'S life."

"Sounds like a familiar song." I often think Fallon will get a belly full and leave.

"No offense, sir, but I don't know too many women who can handle this life."

"I'm not so sure they should have to." Maybe freeing Fallon from the likes of me is a better option than marrying her. "You said you're from Florida?"

"I moved there when I was ten years old."

"What made you decide to join the military?"

"All the war movies my uncle used to play for us when the crowds went home. I wanted to be just like them."

"A boy playing army." I chuckle.

"Yeah, but I love what I do and wouldn't give it up for anyone."

“You and Thorn sound like you could be brothers.”

“Most the brothers I’ve met feel the same way. Why don’t you get a little shut-eye while I drive.”

“Sleeping is not on the agenda.”

CHAPTER 7

NINA

"I've never had guests on this magnificent floating machine before." I sit on the crisp white sofa filled with colorful throw pillows that boast different kinds of sea urchins on them.

"I wouldn't define the people you kidnapped as guests." Fallon scoots close to Sean, who's still heavily sedated. Maxim had to drag him in here.

"Don't be silly, you're my guest." I brush out my wet hair.

"Will you untie me so I can look at him?" She holds out her hands.

"He's fine. Nothing a shower, and a few stitches won't cure." I wave my hand at her.

"I promise not to try to get away." She keeps her hands up.

"Maxim, undo her hands, but don't take your eyes off her," I instruct him.

He snatches a knife from his pocket and cuts her loose. She gets up and tries to get Sean to sit. "Hey, it's Fallon. Sean, can you hear me?" She lifts his eyelid. "What did you give him?"

"Just a little milk." I laugh. "He's been a very bad boy."

"May I have a washcloth to clean his face?" She's inspecting his wound.

I raise a shoulder at Maxim. "Give her one." He hands me his gun while he goes to find a washcloth.

The captain of my yacht enters the room. "Ma'am, the water is still too rough for us to leave."

"Keep the engine's idling and the slightest break in the weather you need to head north."

"Yes, ma'am," he responds and leaves the room.

Maxim comes back in, handing Fallon a plush white washcloth and takes his weapon back.

She takes it from him and walks over to the sink, getting it wet. She returns and holds Sean's head up with one hand and cleans the blood off the side of his face.

"How sweet. Does Derrick know how much you care for his brother? Maybe you chose the wrong man."

"He's family."

"Not yet. You can walk away. All Derrick will ever bring you is a life of danger."

"You're the only danger to me."

"Pity, you're so naive. You'll never be able to satisfy a man like Derrick." I get up and open the thick dark curtains and watch the storm rolling across the water, creating white peaks, causing the yacht to sway back and forth.

"You seem to think you know him. You weren't together very long, and it was under false pretense. You have no idea who he is or what he's capable of now."

"I know he couldn't save your adopted sister."

"Her death was your fault, not his."

"I'm curious. Did you ever want to meet your real parents?"

"My adoptive parents were my real parents. They loved me and gave me a good home and a great life."

"Not everyone can be as lucky as you, if luck is what you want to call it."

She rinses out the cloth and starts again. "Do you have any family?"

"We've all come from someone." I shrug.

"You don't act like a woman that was shown much love."

"Not everyone is capable of love, and not everyone should have children."

"Your parents didn't love you?" She sits on the arm of the couch with the blood-tinged cloth in her hand.

"I'm sure in their own way, they did."

"Where are they?"

"Gone. Why all the questions? Are you trying to psychoanalyze me?"

"Something or someone has made you into a monster."

"Funny, I don't see myself as you proclaim. I'm a woman that knows what she wants and how to get it."

"By kidnapping innocent people, selling them to the highest bidder, or for their body parts? In my book, that makes you worse than a monster."

"A mythical creature, but far be it from what you portray me as." I snort. "People are a means to an end for me. Imagine how happy the recipients are that receive an organ that will save their life."

"At the cost of another human being. That makes them as sick as you are."

I walk over to her and jerk her head back. "You're a weak fool that doesn't deserve what I've given you."

"Given me?"

"That's a story for another day." I let go of her hair. "Get them out of here," I snap at Maxim. "And tie her back up."

He tugs her by the arm to stand and ties her. "I'll lock her up and be back for him." He angles his head at Sean.

He leads her down the stairs, and Sean stirs. "Fallon," he slurs.

"Are you going to be a good boy, or do I need to drug you again?" I run my hand down the uninjured side of his face. His head falls forward. "You really are quite handsome. You'd make a nice plaything for me, but I think you should belong to your brother's girlfriend."

"Fallon," he says again.

Maxim returns and hovers over him.

"Is she secure?"

"Yes."

"Take this one to her, but before you do, give him some more sleepy-time medicine. I don't want to have to deal with him tonight."

He hoists Sean up and drags him away.

I call down to the chef to bring me a plate of food as I walk over to the bar and pour myself a glass of expensive wine. I take the bottle with me and sit out on the covered deck to enjoy the sight of the black clouds rolling over the land. The rain is finally slowing, but the wind is still strong, causing the yacht to rock. I take out my phone and text Derrick.

"*I know you're out there, hunting me. Sweet Fallon's clock is ticking, but the others have less time. If you don't get to them soon, you'll never see them again.*" I hit send and wait for a response.

"*You're my target,*" he sends back.

"*As much as I'd love to see you again, you really should focus on the other woman in your life. I'll give you a hint. If I drink, I die. If I eat, I'm fine.*" Send.

"*What the hell kind of clue is that?*"

"*Want a little more? A group of men kill me so that I don't spark. If you find where they live, you'll see the light.*"

"*I'm tired of your games.*"

"*Come on, handsome, you like the challenge.*" I hit send and hang up. That should keep him busy.

The chef brings my food out to me. "See to it that our guests get a plate." I shoo him off.

I'm not an idiot. I know Derrick will never love me, but I can offer him so much more than love, which doesn't mean anything. He's always pushed me, and he's one determined man. I like that. He's been the only man that's held my interest beyond a few weeks. I'll buy him. Everyone can be bought for the right amount of money, even Cinderella being held captive downstairs. I polish off my glass of wine and food. I wander downstairs and stop at my guest's room. I unlock the door, and Fallon is curled up next to Sean.

"Wouldn't Derrick love this picture." She sits up. "Take his clothes off," I order.

"What?"

"You heard me. Remove his clothes."

"I'm not taking his clothes off."

"What's the matter, haven't you seen a man's junk before? Don't tell me you're a virgin." I laugh.

She bites her lip.

"You really are pathetic. I don't know what Derrick sees in you."

"I'm not letting you bait me." She sits and crosses her arms over her chest.

"In the end, he'll pick me. You weren't raised to be a strong, powerful woman, and that's what he needs." I slam the door and retire to my room for the night. I never sleep more than a couple hours at a time. Before I turn in, I call the captain. "The storm will be ending soon. I want us out ahead of it. Get the engines going and pull out of here now."

CHAPTER 8

THORN

"I know the answer to her riddle," I tell Rebel over the radio. "It's a fire station. Tate's been reading Nina's journal. It's all about her childhood. We're headed there now. She's from Forks, which is only four hours out."

"What else did you find?"

"She had or has a sister. She gave her away."

"Oh my god," Tate says. "She killed her own mother," she reads out of the journal.

"What did she say?" Rebel asks.

Tate links into the conversation. "Her mother was a junkie, and Nina gave her an overdose because she told her she was too stupid to go to college."

"She's more evil than I thought," Rebel responds.

"According to this journal, Nina had a really

rough upbringing. I think she was protecting her sister from the same fate."

"Nina doesn't have a protective bone in her body. She's a total narcissist."

"I think at one time she did. Maybe this was the changing point in her life," Tate says.

"I've chartered a boat. I'm going after Nina, but you have to find Lauryn and your ex-wife. She says they are running out of time."

"Eden, her name is Eden." I don't know why I felt the need to clarify it. "Honor, are you on the horn?"

"Yes."

"Can you get us a chopper so we can get there quicker now that the storm has subsided?"

"I'll pinpoint your location and send one in your direction. I located the fire station, but it's not the one you want because it's operational. She can't be holding them there. I located an abandoned one that was operational during the time frame that Nina would've lived in Forks."

"That's the one we want. Did you find the house she grew up in?"

"Not yet. There are so many areas that are off-grid, and tons of mobile homes tucked into areas that were never tracked."

"Nina mentions walking a couple miles to school every day. Pan out a radius around the elementary school," Tate suggests.

"That shouldn't be too hard. There's only one school in Forks." I can hear Honor's fingers flying over the keyboard.

"From the sounds of it, I'm betting she lived in a run-down mobile home where junkies hid," I tell her.

"I'll keep looking. In the meantime, I'll have a chopper in the air shortly. I'll send you the coordinates where they can land."

"Roger, that. Captain, you have anything else to add?"

"Secure the surrounding area before you move in. If I'm chasing Nina, that means she has other people doing her dirty work. I'm sure she's set a trap for us."

"We'll be on alert."

* * *

Honor has the chopper in the air, and within thirty minutes, we are strapping in our seats. Tate pulls hers tight.

"Don't tell me you don't like helicopters either?" Theo chuckles.

"Hate them."

"Then you're really going to love it when we have to jump out of this thing. There's nowhere to land in Forks, according to Honor's last message."

"Great." Her face turns green.

Within an hour, we're within a couple miles of our target. "When we hit the ground, we'll head due west on foot. We want the element of surprise, and this bird is too loud. It will announce our arrival," I yell over the sound of the blades whirling around. "Get us as low as you can," I tell the pilot.

He descends. Theo goes first. I watch as Tate says a few hail Mary's and jumps. I dart out right after her, landing a few feet from her. We roll and get to our feet running. We don't stop until we're in the trees that line the property of the old run-down firehouse.

"There are two men guarding the front," I whisper to Theo. "I'll make my way around back. You take them out. Tate, when they hit the ground you go in the front, be ready for more to be inside. Theo, stay put in case they radio for backup."

He starts setting up his scope, and I move between the trees to the back. One man is sitting in a chair with his head down and his rifle by his side. Once I hear the all-clear from Theo, I slowly move toward him. The step on the porch creaks, and he lifts his head. I run at him, knocking him over in the chair before he can get his hands on his weapon.

"Don't make me kill you," I say with my arms wrapped around his head, grasping him in a choke-hold. He kicks and tries to break free, but I don't let up. He passes out, and I draw my weapon, opening the back door.

Shots ring out, and I hear Tate telling them not to move. "Where are they?" she asks loudly.

"Fuck off!" one of them yells.

I come up behind him and slam my gun into the side of his head. It knocks him out cold. The other guy puts his hands in the air.

"They're down there," he indicates a door with his head. "But it's booby-trapped. If you go inside the room, you'll trigger an explosive and the room will go up in flames along with the women."

"Then you're going to show me how not to trip it."

"I can't do that. Ms. Pax would kill me."

I press my gun to his temple. "If you don't tell me, I'm going to kill you. Your choice." I lift one shoulder.

"Okay, okay." He raises his hands.

"Lead the way." I follow him. "Theo, how's it looking out there?"

"A black SUV is coming down the road."

"Don't let whoever it is out of the vehicle."

"Copy."

"Tate, stay close behind me. There is no telling what kind of condition they're in." She follows close behind me.

He opens the door, and it leads down a set of wooden stairs. It looks like it used to be a food pantry and storage for their gear.

"There's a wire on the sixth step." He points.

He steps over, and we mimic his walking pattern. "Be careful of the switch on the bottom step. You hit it, and we'll all be dead."

One by one, we clear it, reaching Eden and Lauryn, who are tied up, leaning against two thick water pipes. Neither one of them has their eyes open. I keep my gun in his back. "Check them," I order Tate and hear gunfire exchange outside.

Eden's eyes open, and she looks directly at me. "Thorn," she cries.

"You okay?" I maintain my position.

"Water, we need water. They haven't given us any in days." Her lips are dry.

"Dr. Ruth, wake up." Tate shakes her, but she doesn't arouse.

"Stand over there." I usher him to the other side of the room, blocking his path to the stairs. I squat and untie Eden while Tate continues trying to wake Lauryn and loosening her binds.

"I got her, you get Eden out of here," I order Tate, and we swap places. I cradle Lauryn in my arms. "I've got you," I whisper, but she doesn't stir. My instinct is to press my lips to hers. I hide my fear that maybe we didn't get here soon enough to save her.

The door at the top of the stairs flies open, and a man wearing all black and a mask rushes inside, shooting. Tate and Eden duck down. I place Lauryn on the ground and grab my weapon, returning fire. The other guy in the back of the room runs toward the stairs, and I hear the click the moment his foot hits the trigger. I throw my body over Lauryn when a loud boom goes off, then flames flash up the walls.

The guy that stepped on it crumples to the ground. The man at the top of the stairs falls downward, crashing on the bottom step into the flames.

Theo appears in the doorway at the top. "Get them out of here!" I yell.

Tate helps Eden up, and they make it out the

door. Theo fights the flames, trying to come down. I pick up Lauryn and see a light coming from the back of the room. "There's a window on the far side!" I holler up at Theo, and he darts out.

Smoke and fire are filling in the room. I lay Lauryn on the ground close to the wall and find a piece of wood to break the small window.

"Hand her up." Theo pokes his head through. I cough away the smoke and bend down, lifting her to him headfirst. He lifts her under the arms and pulls her out. I jump up and grab the window sill that's left with shards of glass and blood fills my hands. It's a tight fit, but I manage to maneuver through it.

"Get out of here, this place is going to explode!" Theo runs with Lauryn in his arms back to the tree area, and the fire station explodes, sending me to the ground for cover from flying debris. Once it's done raining down on me, I get up and make it over to them, and it isn't until then that I see blood on Eden's shirt on her left shoulder.

I kneel down and hold pressure.

"She was shot." Tate is digging into her medical bag.

"I'm sorry," Eden whispers, "for the things I did to you."

"Stop talking. You're going to be fine."

I lift my hand to take a look. The bullet went straight through clear of any vital organs. "You're going to be okay. I promise."

"There's still one man out there. Four were in the vehicle. I killed the driver and the passenger on this side. One man dead in the fire station." Theo looks beyond the trees, and a shot rings out, nearly missing him. "Get down!" he shouts.

Tate is pulling her medical kit out. "Dr. Ruth needs fluids." She jabs an IV into a vein.

"We are sitting ducks out here. I'm sure he's called for backup by now." I look around for any kind of shelter. "Over there." I point to a run-down shack a thousand feet out. "Theo, you cover us. Once we're inside, I'll call for a chopper to get us out."

Lauryn's eyes flutter open. "Where are we?" Her voice is hoarse from the dryness.

Tate has a grip on the bag of fluids, flooding it into her veins.

"Do you think you can get them to the shack? Theo and I will cover you," I ask.

She unhooks Lauryn, helping her to her feet. I turn Eden toward me. "When I say run, you go as fast as you can and don't stop until you're inside. Do you understand me?"

She's visibly shaking and clutching her shoulder. "Yes."

I reach in Tate's bag and take out a forty-five. "Ready. Go!" I holler and step out from behind the tree, laying out a path of bullets with Theo. Eden sprints out in front, and Tate and Lauryn stumble along. Tate bends down and picks up Lauryn over her shoulder and moves quickly.

"They're inside. You go, and I'll be right behind you," I order Theo. He gathers up our bags and moves. I maintain my position until he's at the door of the shack. I see him throw the bags inside and position himself on the rickety porch with his rifle.

"Move!" he yells, and I take off in a run.

"He's down," Theo says as I make it to him.

"Let's get inside and assess our wounds." I tuck my weapon into my holster.

Lauryn has color back in her face, and Eden is holding her shoulder. "How is she?" I look directly at Tate.

"We need to get both of them checked out, but they'll be okay."

I connect with Honor. "We need a chopper. Get our coordinates from the satellite and tell me the closest place it can land."

"Roger. Checking now," she responds.

"Where's Captain Rebel? Has he located our target?"

"He's headed in her direction."

"Report back to him that Dr. Ruth and the other hostage have been recovered. We'll bring them back with us. Make sure a medical team meets us at headquarters."

"We'll do. I'm sending you the pickup location. Landing estimated time arrival is thirty minutes," Honor spouts off.

"Copy." I look at my phone to assess the distance to the landing spot. "If you didn't shoot out the engine in the SUV, we could make it to these coordinates the same time the chopper will land," I tell Theo.

"Only one way to find out. Cover me," he says, and I follow him outside.

He pulls the body of the driver out of the seat and climbs inside. The engine starts, and he drives it through the grass and around several trees to park it.

"Did you see any signs of anyone?" he asks when he gets out.

"No, but that doesn't mean they're not headed this way. I'll keep watch. Get the girls in the car."

He darts into the shack and brings them out. Tate gets in the middle up front, and I get in the back with Lauryn and Eden in the middle. Theo jumps behind the wheel. I hand him my phone with the GPS coordinates.

"You okay?" I ask Eden. "Did they hurt you?"

"Not physically no, but I overheard one of them talking about selling me and that I'd bring them a lot of money. I was so scared." She lays her head on my shoulder, and I gaze over at Lauryn.

"How about you. Did they hurt you?"

She shakes her head and looks out the window. "There's a truck coming." She points.

It's headed directly toward her door. "Floor it, Theo!" My hand lands on his shoulder. He speeds up, and the truck clips the back end of the SUV, jolting us all to the side.

Theo rights the vehicle. "Put your seat belts on." I reach for Eden's and strap her in, then climb into the back of the vehicle, kicking out the window with my boot.

"Get down!" Eden and Lauryn duck their heads. Tate rolls down her window and aims behind us.

When they see our weapons, the truck puts distance between us. "There are four men inside. Don't slow down and find the quickest way to get us to the chopper."

Theo cuts through a wooded area, barely making

it between trees. The truck follows us and picks up speed. We're bouncing up and down so hard, I can't get a good shot off.

"When we get there, nobody get out of this vehicle until I say so. Tate, I'll hold them off from here. You get the women in the chopper. Theo, get us as close as you can."

He nods and swerves out on to the two-lane road. When the truck following us does the same, I blow out one of their tires. It slows them, but they keep moving. "That will buy us a few seconds," I say. "How much further?"

As I ask the question, I hear the chopper in the air, heading to the pickup point. "We'll be there before he can land," Theo responds and jerks the SUV into an open area. He drives around the field, allowing the chopper to set the bird down. "Hold on, I'm getting us closer." He gets a safe distance away then swings the SUV sideways, so the driver's side is away from the chopper. He opens his door, stepping out, firing his weapon.

"Go, Tate, get them out of here." They rush out, and I climb over the seat, helping Theo hold them off.

They come to a stop, and all four get out, taking cover and returning fire. I take out one, and Theo hits the driver. Another truck speeds up behind them, almost running over their own man. He rolls, and I get a direct hit. Theo takes down the other one, and then we both focus on the other truck that moved beyond us, closer to the chopper. We take off on foot. Theo shoots the driver in the temple. The other man is running, shooting his weapon in the direction of the chopper. I clip him in the back, and he falls flat. Theo jumps in the chopper, and I'm right behind him.

"Make sure they're strapped in," I yell over the blades. I climb in the front and see the pilot's head dangling downward. There's blood splattered and dripping from his mouth. I move quickly to unstrap him and lift him into the other seat.

"The pilot's dead!" Eden screams. "Who's going to fly us out of here?" Fear is embedded on her face.

"I am." I buckle in and make adjustments before I lift us off the ground.

CHAPTER 9

THORN

"Damn, from the sounds of things, I didn't think I'd see you guys again." Lawson slaps me on the back when I walk through the headquarters door.

"Are the medics here?"

"Yeah, they're in the war room waiting."

I turn toward Theo. "Bring Eden to them. I'll take Dr. Ruth up to her office and get her settled and be back down to check on Eden."

He nods and leads her away. She looks over her shoulder at me but doesn't say anything. Lauryn is quiet as we ride up the loud elevator.

"We passed my floor," she says, biting her lip.

"I know. I'm taking you to my apartment."

"I don't think that's such a good idea." She tries to stand tall but wobbles.

I catch her and wrap my arm around her waist. "I'm not giving you a choice. You need to lay down, and if you go to your office, you'll want to work."

She presses her lips together. "I'm too exhausted to argue with you."

"Good," I say as the door opens and usher her into my place. As soon as the door closes, I crush her to me. "God, I thought you were dead when I first saw you tied to the water pipe."

A soft sob falls on my shoulder. "I've never been so scared in my entire life. I don't know how you do this job."

I put my hands on either side of her face and place soft kisses on her cheeks, nose, and forehead. "I do it to save lives like yours, but in all honesty, I've never been terrified until today." I dip down and kiss her lips like I wanted to earlier. For a brief moment, she gets lost in our tongues clashing together, then she pushes away from me.

"We can't do this." She wipes away a tear. "This doesn't change anything."

"It does whether you like it or not. You and I've had miles and years come between us, yet we both know there's still something that neither one of us can deny. I almost lost you before we've had a chance to figure it out. We owe it to ourselves to explore the feelings we have for one another."

She pulls away. "It doesn't matter how we feel. Neither one of us are going to give up our careers for the other, and I won't have you sacrifice yourself for me again. We've been down that road."

I grab her by the arm and hold her against me. "You let me worry about that. I gave you up once, and I won't do it again. All these years and I've never felt for anyone the way I feel about you. I thought I had let it go until I saw you in this building. One look at you and this heart of mine that I thought was dead, started beating again. It feels too damn good to stop it now."

She steps away again. "You don't think I've felt the same way all these years? It doesn't change the fact that there is no redemption for the two of us."

"You're wrong about that."

"I've spent several days with Eden locked up in a room with her. Half the time, they put a gag in my mouth so that I couldn't speak. Nina told them I was dangerous with my words and that I'd try to trick them. So for hours, I got to listen to Eden talk. She made her mistakes, but she was right about one thing."

"What's that?"

"After you and I were together, she never had a chance to work her way back into your life. She said I stole your heart."

"You did, but if she wouldn't have slept with another man, you couldn't have stolen it from her. I could've forgiven her anything, but not cheating."

"She was lonely."

"Are you making excuses for her?" I raise a brow, and my voice deepens.

"No. I'm only saying, now that I've been doing this for a while, I see it."

I step up close to her. "You've been lonely." It's not a question. I can see it in her eyes.

She nods. "Yes. But we're not talking about me. Eden was young and didn't know how to handle a life she admittedly didn't want. She loved you enough to try it, and it left her in an empty house for far too long."

I move away, taking her hand and leading her to the couch. She sits, and I walk into the kitchen and grab two bottles of water, handing her one.

"It took me a lot of years to realize my marriage was wrong to begin with. You're right. She didn't want to be married into the military, and I forced her hand because I thought we could make it work." I sit next to her. "The problem was, I loved my job more than I loved my wife. It's not something I'm proud of, but it doesn't change the facts. After you left, the year I spent with her, I grew up. I tried to forgive her for the affair and the baby, but I'd built a wall that there was no way she was climbing over. I saw her for the first time and realized that I never really loved her. I liked the idea of being settled down after moving from place to place all my teenage years. She was sweet, beautiful, and for some reason, crazy about my sorry ass." I take a swig of my water. "She thought that entire year that I'd forget about being a SEAL." I chuckle. "The only two things I thought about were my brothers in arms, and you. Once my agreement was up with Eden, I looked you up. You were in Germany by then. I'd read that you'd been promoted several times and had landed in a job with a SEAL team. You followed your dreams, and I chose to move on with mine, erasing Eden from my life."

"I looked you up too. You were with your platoon and had just come back from a mission in Afghanistan. You looked happy in the picture online."

I stand.

"Where are you going?"

"I'm going to check on Eden and make sure she gets home to her husband and children. I'll send a medic up to see you." I walk to the door. "This thing between us is far from over." I close the door behind me and take the stairs down to the war room. Eden is sitting in a chair, and the medic is dressing her shoulder.

"Is the patient well enough to travel?" I ask him. "She needs to go home to her family."

"Yes. I'll send her with some antibiotics and pain meds."

I pick up the phone on the table. "Honor, get a flight for Eden to go home and get her family on the horn." I hang up.

"Would you give us a minute," Eden asks the medic.

"Apartment 4. Dr. Ruth is waiting," I tell him.

I pull out a chair and sit when the room is clear.

"Thank you for saving me." Eden's lip quivers.

"I'm afraid you knowing me is what put you in danger in the first place."

"That woman...Nina, she's pure evil."

"Yes, she is."

"Does she really sell women?"

"Yes, she does."

"You're going to stop her?"

"Our team is going to stop her."

"I see it now." She trails her fingers down my face.

"See what?" My brows draw together.

"Why this job is so important and why a man like you can't resist it. You were right to choose it over me. You save people."

"I was wrong to bring you into a life you didn't want, and for that, I'm sorry." She blinks her eyes, chasing away tears. "Are you happy?" I ask after a long moment of looking into her eyes.

"Yes. I'm married to a man that adores me, and we have two beautiful little girls."

"Then I guess it all worked out for you." I give her a half smile.

"What about you? You still love her, don't you?"

"Lauryn? I do feel something for her, but we both love our careers more."

"I ruined that for you, didn't I?"

"I'm sure things would've worked out differently, but I still wouldn't have given up my life. I'm a selfish bastard." I chuckle.

Honor opens the door. "Eden, I have your husband on the phone."

She stands. "I saw the way you looked at her. You may think yourself a bastard, but do yourself a favor and trust what you feel for her." She squeezes my shoulder as she walks by me.

For the first time, all my anger at her is gone. I get up. "Eden."

She turns around.

"If you ever need anything, you know where to find me."

She walks back over and kisses me on the cheek. "You're not as much of a bastard as you think. In fact, I think you're a good man under all the bravado."

"I wouldn't go that far." I laugh, and follow her out. Honor tucks her into Rebel's office to talk to her husband.

"Anything on Rebel?"

"The last connection I received from him was that he was making his way on foot to this location." She points to her computer screen. "Nina has a yacht in the water."

"He's going to need backup. Get me a chopper."

"I'm going with you." Theo walks into the room and chimes into the conversation.

"Like hell you are! It's my turn to get into the action. You stay here and babysit the women." Mad Dog bursts into the conversation.

"Babysit?" Honor's voice rises.

"I didn't mean you. I can't sit here and standby anymore." He rakes his hand over his short stubble of hair.

"I'll stay behind." Theo tucks Fiona into his side.

"I'm with Honor. I'm pissed off about the babysitting comment. I want to help too." Fiona pulls away from him. "I'm a lot tougher than I look, and I've survived way worse." She places her hands on her hips.

"For Pete's sake, would you apologize to the women before we have a mutiny on our hands," I tell Mad Dog.

"I'm sorry, ladies. I only wanted to keep all of you safe."

Tate runs into the room. "You won't believe what I found in Nina's journal."

"Did you find anything that will lead us to where she is headed?"

"No, but..."

"Then it can wait," I cut her off. "Mad Dog and I are headed to the airfield. Honor, keep glued to your monitor. Theo, see to it that Eden is escorted to her plane and all the way back home."

"I'll get ahold of Commander Lukas to assign a patrol to her," he responds.

"Perfect." I turn to Lawson. "Dr. Ruth is in my apartment upstairs being seen by a medic. Under no circumstances is she to leave headquarters. If you have to lock her in my room, you have my permission."

"In your room, huh?" He winks at Honor, and she purses her lips at him.

"Is there something going on between the two of you?" Part of me hopes he answers yes because it would take the heat off me and Lauryn for Lawson to be messing around with Rebel's assistant.

"No," he answers, but I don't believe him.

"Tate, you keep digging into that journal and let me know the minute you find anything that will lead us to her."

"Yes, sir." She hands an envelope to Honor. "Maybe you'll find this interesting," she mumbles and leaves the room.

* * *

"Did you see that explosion?" Mad Dog points out into the dark water.

"That's the location that Honor pinpointed Nina's yacht," I respond.

"If anyone was on that boat, they're dead." He

pulls out a pair of binoculars, trying to see through the darkness.

I increase the speed of the chopper toward the bright orange inferno burning in the ocean. "Let's hope Rebel and Remington weren't on it."

CHAPTER 10

REBEL

"There she is." I point out into the darkness as a slow-moving yacht making its way out into the ocean.

The chopper pilot angles the nose toward the boat. "I'm flying in dark," he says, turning off the lights on the outside. "We don't want to give her any warning."

"The wind should drown out the sound of this bird." Remington is gearing up to jump out.

"Drop us a thousand feet out. I'm not risking her hearing us coming for her. We'll swim in and find a way to get onto the yacht.

"Water's freezing, sir," the pilot adds.

"I'm sure we've been in worse conditions." I recall a mission that we jumped into the icy arctic waters. It took me days to not be chilled to the bone.

"I've been in waters so cold my balls completely disappeared." Remington chuckles.

"We're in position, sir." The chopper hovers over the dark waters of the Pacific Ocean. I unstrap and pick up my gear. Remington salutes me and plunges into the water. I leap right behind him.

Cold water chases over my body, nearly taking my breath away as I make it to the surface. The radio buzzes in my ear as I begin swimming. I grab Remington's foot to stop his forward motion.

"Honor, can you hear me?"

Static... "Fallon"... static... "letter"...

"I can't hear you, Honor. Whatever it is, take care of it. We're boarding Nina's yacht."

I motion for Remington to move. It's a hard swim in the choppy ocean water to catch the slow-moving yacht. Waves are still heavy from the storm that's moved further inland. As we make it to the platform on the back, I hear the sound of a chopper coming from the other direction. Two men guarding the stern of the boat take off to the bow, leaving one heavily armed man in place. He's dressed in all black, wearing a bulletproof vest, carrying a high-powered weapon.

I point two fingers at my eyes, then at Remington for him to keep watch. I silently climb on the lower deck and wait for the guard to walk to the port side of the boat. Remington moves to the deck, and the knife on his fatigues clanks against the metal ladder. I adjust my position, gazing over the edge of the boat to see the guard level his weapon and head toward the noise he heard.

Remington slides back into the water and under the boat. The man peers over the side. I slink onto the deck, coming up behind him. He turns his head when he hears me. I ball my hand, punching him in the lower back. It only slows him for a second. We wrestle for control of his weapon, both of our fists gripping onto it. I drive my knee into his crotch, forcing him to move backward against the wall of the boat. Remington jumps out of the water and wraps his arm around the guy's neck. Before I can pry the weapon out of his hand, it goes off next to my ear, forcing me to let go, grasping my head from the sharp, ringing pain.

His combat boots fly in the air as Remington drags him off the boat with him. Remington manages to latch onto the side, and the man is dragged deep into the water with his vest weighing him down. I reach my hand out and pull my man up onto the deck.

"The chopper has landed on the front bow of the yacht. We need to stop it from taking off. You make your way to the bow. I'll go inside." We part ways, and I move to the door on the back of the boat. I step inside with my weapon drawn. Water drips off my clothing onto the polished floor. The large room is empty other than furniture and pictures on the wall. There's an envelope on the bar with my name on it. I shove it into my pocket and walk down the hall, opening each door, looking inside. I make my way down to the next level. The first room I come to has blood on the sheets, and Fallon's scent lingers in the air.

"Fallon," I whisper. "I'll fucking kill you, Nina." I rein in my emotions and continue searching until I'm sure Fallon and Sean are not on board.

Shots ring out, and I run up the stairs to the top deck. The door is locked from the outside. I can only hear the sound of the blades swirling and feel the shift of the yacht as the chopper lifts off the deck. I fire a shot at the locked door and rush through it. I run toward the leg of the chopper, but it's already too far off the deck to reach it. I look up to see Nina waving down at me. I can't see past her to tell if anyone else is in there with her. She blows me a kiss then drags a lifeless body toward her for me to see. It's Sean. I don't want to take out the pilot and risk killing him. I aim at the part where the blades meet the chopper, but the bullet ricochets and the pilot yanks the chopper higher in the air. I look around the deck of the boat and see Remington getting to his feet. He's holding his head, and blood is dripping down his hand.

"They knew we were here. One of her men jumped me from behind," he says, as he reaches my side.

I cover my ear. "Honor!"

"I can hear you," she responds. "Turn our chopper around. Tell him to pick us up on the yacht."

"Thorn is in a chopper headed your way, but I need..."

"Now, Honor!" I shout

"Do you hear that?" Remington asks as the chopper gets further away.

My ear still aches from the sound of the weapon going off next to my face. "Hear what?"

"Something is ticking, sir. Get off the boat. Now!" he yells, and we both take off running. I dive off the starboard side; Remington off the port side.

Before I'm submerged in the cold water, I hear the explosion. I dive deep to avoid the flying debris. Orange and yellow flames fill the water above me. I hold my breath, swimming out further to clear it and come up gasping for air. Black smoke hangs on the water, making it hard to see anything in the darkness other than what's left of the boat on fire.

I swim back under the flames, closer to the sinking yacht. A captain's hat is floating in the water. Not far from it, I see a body facedown.I swim over and roll the captain's body over. Half his face is missing, and he gasps, spilling blood into the water.

"Help me," he gurgles before the light leaves his eyes.

"Remington!" I yell in the darkness. A hand lands on my shoulder, and I turn to find the face of the guard that was thrown off the back of the boat. He lands a hard punch to my jaw, sinking me backward. Then he's on top of me, holding me under with his hands around my throat. I keep one hand on his, and with the other, I feel for my knife tucked into the side of my pants. I rip it out and thrust it into his side. He instantly releases me. I come up for air, and he drifts off into the bloody water.

I blink back the smoke and the darkness to see someone swimming in my direction.

"You okay, sir?" Remington treads water a few feet from me.

"No! I'm fucking pissed off that we were that close to Nina, and she got away again." I look up and see the chopper circling back in our direction, taunting me. It makes a few rounds and then hovers over us for a few moments then takes off toward the north. Out of the east, I see a light angled down into the water, headed in our direction.

"We need to get on the other side of those flames," I tell Remington. We both dive under and swim out toward the chopper. I can only hope it's Thorn.

When it gets closer, I know it's a military chopper. A rope is tossed out, and I can see Mad Dog on the other end of it.

"You go first," I order Remington. He starts the climb, and I hear another set of blades spinning. Nina's chopper has turned around and is coming straight for ours. I grab onto the rope and hold on for dear life when Thorn swerves out of the way, jerking the chopper up at the same time. I hear artillery going off, but I can't tell which direction it's coming from. Thorn levels the bird out, and Remington continues to climb. I inch up a few feet, and the chopper dips, dragging me into the water, trailing close to the flames. I don't let go, knowing he'll pull me back up. When he does, the wind and cold air rip through me. Remington has made it in the chopper, and I feel the rope being wrenched upward. Weapons ring out again, and Nina's chopper takes off north into the dark sky.

I climb as the rope tugs closer to the chopper. Mad Dog's large hand reaches down and drags me inside. I lay flat on my back, trying to catch my breath. "Go after her," I say between gasps.

Thorn makes a hard, sharp right turn.

"Fuck!" I hear Thorn curse.

I get to my knees. "What is it?"

"The GPS system just went down. I can only assume that Nina is blocking it. I can't track her in the dark."

"Honor, are you hearing this?"

"Yes. Our systems are down, too, sir."

"What the hell kind of connections does she have that she can block a satellite feed?"

"An expensive one or someone that owes her a big favor," Mad Dog answers.

"Honor, have Tate go over her list of people that received organs from geNetics. Look for someone that works in aerospace engineering."

"She's pulling it up now, sir."

"We're going to head in the same direction she did and hope they didn't change their course."

"Sir, I need to tell you about a letter..."

"Found him." I hear Tate over the radio. "David Spencer. He received a double lung transplant from geNetics. He's the head of three satellite stations. One covering the Pacific Northwestern region of the United States."

"Find him and shut him down. Bring him in for questioning."

"Sir, I..." The radio goes dead.

Honor mentioning a letter reminds me of the one I shoved in my pocket. I pull it out soaking wet. I carefully open it and unfold the fragile paper. The ink has bled through it, making it hard to read. I can make out the words cat and mouse and something about Sean.

"Give me your phone!" I snap at Mad Dog, and he hands it to me. I take a snapshot of the letter and send it to Honor. She'll know by the looks of it that it needs deciphering.

I get off the metal floor and buckle into the copilot seat.

"Sorry about the rough climb, sir." Thorn looks over at me.

"You did fine. You've got some amazing skills in that she didn't kill us all with that move."

"We thought you both were dead when we saw the yacht explode."

"We were lucky that Remington heard the ticking when he did." I glance over my shoulder at him, and he smiles.

"Saved both our asses," he admits.

"Dr. Ruth and Eden are safe. We'll get Fallon and your brother back, too, sir," Thorn says, flatly.

"The women are okay?"

"Our medic treated Eden, and she's on her way back home with a military escort, thanks to Commander Lukas."

"And Lauryn?"

"They're keeping her at headquarters, giving her fluids, but she'll recover." I see a deep line crease in his forehead.

"Anything you want to tell me?"

"No, sir." His jaw flexes a few times.

"When this is all over with, you and I will talk." I point at him.

"Yes, sir."

CHAPTER 11

NINA

"You need to vacate your position. It won't take them long to find out who cut the satellite feed, and they'll come after you. And you know what will happen to you if you implicate me." I hang up. Spencer owes me his life, he'll never talk. I look behind me to see Sean stirring next to Fallon.

Maxim starts prepping a syringe.

"Hold off on that. I may need to toss his ass from the chopper if Derrick gets too close." I don't want to kill him if I don't have to. If he's awake, he'll have a fighting chance. He's nothing more than a tool for me to snare Derrick.

"Your boyfriend is proving to be one lucky son of a bitch. I can't believe he cleared the yacht before my bomb went off." Maxim snarls.

"He's not her boyfriend," Fallon says.

"Oh, sister, he's so much more than you think."

"I'm not your sister," she snarks.

"I think someone is overly sensitive."

"Where are we?" Sean's eyes are glazed over, looking around. "Fallon," he says.

She reaches over and holds his hand. "She's had you drugged. Don't try to fight her."

"Are you okay?" he asks her.

"I will be once this is over with." She glares at me with so much heat I feel my skin burn.

"Does my brother have any idea where we are?" he asks her.

"I've left him breadcrumbs to follow, and he's a smart man," I answer for her.

"You want him to find us?" Fallon's eyes light up. "You know he'll kill you when he catches you."

I tap my finger to my chin. "Do I? Hmmm...I'm betting he won't."

"You're going to lose that bet," she hisses.

"If he doesn't, I will." Sean's gaze cuts through me.

"You're not the killing type." I laugh. "You're the sweet one, not a soldier."

He jerks at his binds, and Maxim levels a gun at him.

"That's where you're wrong. I'll kill for my family."

"Boss lady, there's a chopper flying blind toward us. He's catching speed," the pilot says.

"It's time to have a little more fun with Derrick." I unbuckle and get in the back. "You get ready to shoot at them," I order Maxim, "but make sure you don't kill him. If you get a good aim, take out one of his men."

I drag Sean off the ground. "Time to use my pawn." He fights against me, trying to shrug out of my grasp. Fallon sticks her foot out, tripping me. I smack my chin hard on the metal floor, pissing me off. I roll over, and Maxim has a gun aimed at Sean's temple and a fist in Fallon's hair, yanking it back.

I wipe the blood from my chin and stand. "If she tries anything again, kill her," I order him. I pull a gun out of a bag and stick it in Sean's chest. "Move." I push him to the open door. "Slow down, let him get closer," I shout over my shoulder to the pilot.

I turn to see Maxim hit Fallon with the butt of his weapon, and she crumples to the ground. "She won't be giving us any more trouble." He stands over her with an evil smile.

I hear the chopper blades before I see them. Maxim takes aim, and I see Derrick pointing a high-powered weapon back at him. I push Sean to the edge and hold him by the shirt collar. I look down over his shoulder into the black water. The pilot flies us within forty feet of the ocean. Neither men shoot their weapons but hold steady.

"When I say the word, you fly this baby up as fast as you can and get the hell out of here," I yell to the pilot.

I move Sean to the side so Derrick can get a view of Fallon on the floor. I see the anger fill his face even from this distance. I lift one hand and wave at him, then shove Sean as hard as I can out of the chopper. "Now," I yell.

The pilot jerks upward and increases his speed at the same time. I look back to see Derrick's chopper has slowed, and they're circling with a light over the water, looking for Sean. I sit on the floor next to Fallon, waiting for her to wake up. I can't stop myself from brushing a wisp of hair from her face. "Please don't make me kill you," I whisper.

She moves slowly, rubbing the side of her head. When her eyes finally open, she's frantic.

"Where's Sean?" She tries to stand, but I yank her to the ground.

"He went for a swim."

"Oh, god, no!" She starts to cry.

"You have one chance to make this all go away. I'll give myself up and never try to harm Derrick or his men again."

"What is it you want?"

"You'll walk away from him, never to see him again. If you do, I'll come back with a vengeance and kill all of them."

"I'm not going to walk away. He'll find you and end this with you six feet under."

I laugh. "Don't say I didn't give you a chance. His life is in your hands."

"Is this really about him, or is it something else?" She straightens her body against the wall, trying to psychoanalyze me.

"That's something you'll have to figure out before it's too late." I raise my shoulder nonchalantly.

"If you're going to kill me, just do it! I'm tired of your games."

"If I wanted you dead, I would've placed my aim a little higher." I point to her stomach.

"Then tell me what it is you want!" she screams.

"I want what I deserve." I purse my lips together before they can quiver, showing any sign of emotion.

"You deserve death for the things you've done. Besides, I thought your only motivation was money, and you have plenty of it."

I let my head fall back. "I do, but I find myself wanting something else, or should I say someone else."

"Rebel," she says.

"I want a life I never had." I look at her, longing for our lives to be switched.

"What was your life like that turned you so evil?" she asks.

"Hell. It was a living hell. My father died in his sleep from an overdose. He laid in the bed two days before my mother came out of her drug-induced stupor and realized he was dead. I was a child and thought he was sleeping." I'd only ever written these words in my journal; saying them out loud makes my stomach turn.

She reaches over and touches my arm, and I stare at her hand. "I'm so sorry," she whispers. My gaze travels to her eyes, and she looks so sincere.

"After he died, my mother needed to make money, so she became a whore, dragging all kinds of men through our house. When I turned thirteen, she decided I was old enough to earn my own keep." The words are out of my mouth before I realize my own admission.

"That's terrible." I see pity in her eyes, and it unnerves me.

I stand abruptly. "She got what she deserved in the end."

"You killed her, didn't you?" Her mouth hangs open.

"You don't get to judge me for the things I've done. You've no idea what it was like growing up in that hellhole. You were lucky to be adopted by parents who adored you, but they made you weak." I squat in front of her. "You don't get a man like Derrick." I brush a piece of hair out of her face.

"And yet, I'm the one he loves." A snarky grin covers her face. And that fragment of a connection I was feeling for her is gone.

"We'll see who he chooses in the end. A life with a woman that can give him everything or a woman that doesn't even know who she really is." I raise a shoulder.

"I know who I am, and he loves me, not you."

"You're so damn naive." I wave her off.

"Where are we going?" she asks.

"Home." I take my seat in the front of the chopper. I close my eyes and visions of my childhood that I've tried to forget plays out before me. Wishing my life to be different doesn't change anything. It's made me who I am. Evil, some may say, but a strong, focused woman, taking what I want out of life. So why has what I wanted suddenly changed? Why do I need Derrick? Is it because of her? I gave her a life, and she has what's mine. He's the only man I've ever come close to feeling what love could be like. Am I willing to sacrifice more to get what I want? The answer is yes. I guess that does make me evil.

"We're thirty minutes out, and there's a car waiting for you," the pilot says, jerking me out of my thoughts.

"Tell them to keep watch. Once Derrick has pulled his brother out of the water, he'll come after us."

CHAPTER 12

THORN

"There he is!" Rebel points out into the water.

I maneuver the chopper so the light is beaming on Sean. He's floating face up, but he's not moving.

"Sir, you take over the chopper, I'll go down." I start unbuckling, and he takes the controls.

"He's my brother. I'll go!" he snaps.

"That's exactly why you need to let me do it, sir." I ignore his order and get out of the pilot seat, picking up the rope and some gear.

"I'll go," Mad Dog growls.

"I don't have time to argue with either one of you." I push him aside.

Remington fastens clips to himself. "I'm going in with you."

Rebel takes over the chopper, moving us closer to the water. Ripples from the blades pushing the water start to form around Sean, splashing into his face. "That's close enough," I yell. "We don't have a basket to lift him, so I'll fasten him to me." I clip hooks to my uniform and pull a rope through them. Then I take the thicker rope and throw it off the edge, dangling feet from the water. "I'm going in," I say seconds before I plunge into the ocean. Remington jumps right behind me. I surface, catching my breath that the cold water stole, swimming over to Sean, hoping like hell he's still alive.

"Sean!" I grasp onto him. His eyes open, but he doesn't speak. "I've got you, man." I tie the rope around his waist, and Remington carefully supports his head. Blood pours from his ears, and I know I have to move quickly. I attach him to me and motion for Rebel to move closer. As the rope drags the water, I grab on. Mad Dog starts pulling us up, leaving Remington in the ocean. Sean gurgles the water from his lungs as we lift higher.

"I can't hear anything," he rasps.

I tug him closer to me so that he knows I got him. As soon as I can reach the ledge of the chopper, I pull him and myself up with the help of Mad Dog dragging us inside. I unfasten Sean and lay him flat on the floor of the chopper. His eyes drift closed, and he passes out. Mad Dog works on getting Remington out of the water.

"We've got to get him to the hospital." Rebel glances over his shoulder at me.

"Get on the radio with Honor. Tell her to call Dr. Ashe Manning. Tell him to meet us at the main Portland Hospital. Have her ask him how long it will take him to get there."

I nod. "Honor, can you hear me?" I yell over the noise of the blades and cover one ear to listen.

"I'm here."

"We've got Sean. He's badly injured, and we're flying him to the Portland Hospital. Get clearance for us to land. Captain says to call Dr. Ashe Manning."

"He's a neurosurgeon. The best in the country," Rebel says loudly.

"Neurosurgeon," I repeat.

"MTA Crisis Division," Rebel adds.

"He says he's with the MTA Crisis Division." I pass the information on to Honor.

"Found him," she says.

"Tell him Sean needs his help. He'll come." Rebel increases the speed of the chopper.

"Evidently, he knows Sean. Tell him he needs him."

"Will do." Honor disconnects.

"He's not breathing," Mad Dog says and feels for a pulse. He shakes his head, and Remington starts chest compressions.

"Don't you fucking die on me!" Rebel hollers over his shoulder.

After two rounds, we have him back. The radio beeps in my ear.

"You're clear to land on the rooftop. Tell Captain Rebel that Dr. Manning was just boarding a plane in Seattle. He'll meet you in Portland."

"Roger that," I respond. I watch over Sean, whose breathing is shallow, until we've landed. A medical team meets us and loads him on the gurney.

A man dressed in blue scrubs walks up to Rebel. "I'm Dr. Hayden. Dr. Manning called me and asked me to cover for him until he gets here." Rebel shakes his hand. "How far out is he?"

The doctor glances at his watch. "His plane should land in thirty minutes."

Rebel turns to Mad Dog, "Get a car. Meet him at the airport."

Without a word, Mad Dog leaves the rooftop. Rebel turns toward me and Remington. "You two find out where Nina's chopper was heading and go after her."

"I'll get on the horn with Honor and see if she got our satellite feed back up." I follow him inside, and the doctor and his team disappear behind double doors with Sean in tow.

Rebel paces the waiting room, wearing a path in the carpet, and I call Honor. "Have you gotten us back online with the satellite feed?"

"Yes. They're tracking between Oil City and La Push, Washington."

"Get the map pulled up," I bark at Remington, who's been leaning against the wall.

He locates the area on the map. "Forks," he says like he recognizes the name.

"You know this area?"

He nods.

"What's in Forks, Washington?" I ask Honor.

"Nina is from there. We've been trying to locate an exact position, but the place is so remote in some areas that we haven't been able to pinpoint it."

Remington snatches the phone out of my hand. "Tell me what you have?" His eyes grow wide as he listens, and Rebel stops his pacing, making his way in our direction.

"I know this location," Remington says.

Rebel grabs his shoulder. "How do you know?"

His throat bobs as if he's swallowed something hard. "I was born there."

"I thought you were from Florida?" Rebel's brows draw tightly together.

"I consider Florida my home. This was a pit stop into a nightmare for me."

"Did you know Nina?"

"If the information that Honor has is correct, she lived down the dirt road from me. It used to be a small trailer park off-grid. Nothing but druggies and prostitutes lived there. My father owned the meth lab that her parents used to buy from."

"Can you locate it from the air?"

"Sure, but you can't land anywhere near there. It's all forest."

A big man in a gray T-shirt and a pair of faded jeans bursts through the door and walks straight toward Rebel.

"Derrick. It's been a while," he says, sticking out his hand.

"Thanks for coming, Ashe."

"I'd do anything for Sean, and you know it. I'm just glad I was on this side of the country when you called."

"How's Aedon?"

"Still putting up with my sorry ass." He chuckles. Then he grows serious. "Dr. Hayden called me as soon as Sean arrived. He has him in the operating room waiting on me. As soon as I'm done, I'll come find you here." He walks backward as he talks until he gets to the double doors.

"How do you know him?"

"Sean lived in New York for a brief period of time. He went to college out there to learn business, and he bartended on the side. The med school students used to hang out there. He and Sean became friends. He sobered him up many times. He's the best in his field and has one hell of a wife. Enough about that. I need to stay here for Sean, and the two of you need to get your asses to Forks and rescue Fallon." He slaps me on the shoulder and grabs the phone from my hand, putting it on speaker.

"Honor. Remington knows this place. Get him and Thorn wings."

"Sir, there's something else you should know. I've been trying to tell you."

"What is it?"

"The journal that Tate found at the building in Seattle, there was a letter of DNA testing inside of it."

"So what? She ran geNetics. I'm sure she has all kinds of test results."

"Sir, it was a sample from Fallon."

"I don't understand."

"Fallon's bloodline matches that of Nina's."

"What are you saying?" Rebel looks like his head is spinning.

"I'm saying that Nina and Fallon are related. In the journal, Nina talks about a sister that she left at a fire station."

"It can't be," he utters in disbelief.

"I remember my father telling me there used to be two children that lived there. He said he thought maybe the baby died. The parents didn't want either one of the girls, and the baby disappeared." Remington is scratching his head as he speaks.

"Fuck," Rebel says.

"That doesn't make any sense. Why would Nina want to hurt Fallon if they're sisters?" I look at him, and he has the same look of confusion that I have.

"I don't know, possibly out of some twisted jealousy." He snaps his fingers. "She always said that Fallon looked like her."

"Do you think she knew from the beginning?" I ask.

"The letter is dated not long after Fallon was taken the first time," Honor interjects.

"When she was being tested to help her sister," Rebel adds.

"Wait, I'm lost." Remington scratches his head again.

"It's a long story. The short of it is, Fallon's adopted sister needed a kidney transplant, and she wanted to be a donor."

"And she sent a sample off to Nina's company." The lights go off in Remington's eyes.

Rebel touches the end of his nose. "Bingo."

"Fallon has no idea," I say, stating the obvious.

"You have to get her back before she finds out. I don't want Nina being the one that tells her. I'm not sure she can handle that kind of news. In fact, I'm not sure I ever want her to know the truth. We already have orders to take Nina out. You make sure that happens before she has a chance to tell Fallon." He points at me as he spouts off orders.

"One more thing, sir," Honor says. "Nina wrote in her journal that she killed her own mother with an overdose of drugs. I wouldn't put anything past her when it comes to Fallon."

"Shit. The story keeps getting worse. Let Thorn

know when you have wheels set up." He ends the conversation.

We all sit in the waiting room chairs. Remington studies the map, and Rebel's hand grips the arm of the chair as if he wants to crush it. Silence hangs between all of us as we sit and wait for word on Sean.

Finally, the door swings open, and Dr. Manning comes out.

"Sean will recover, but he's got a long road ahead of him. I was able to stop the bleeding in his brain, but I couldn't repair his eardrums. I'm sorry, but he's deaf, and I'm not sure what the long-term effects will be for him. He lost some mobility in his left leg, but I think in time he'll get it back. We won't know for sure until he fully wakes up, and I can assess him."

Rebel hangs his head and wipes his eyes.

"I'm sorry. I did all I could for him."

"I know you did. Thanks for coming. I'm sure he wouldn't still be here if you didn't." He sniffs back his emotions.

"At minimum, he would've been in a wheelchair for the rest of his life. I wish I could've done more for his hearing, but the impact shattered his eardrums. I'll stick around for a few days and watch him recover."

"Thanks, I appreciate it." He sticks out his hand to him.

"You look like shit. Why don't you go get some rest. I'm going to keep him comfortable until morning. He'll never know you're here."

"I've got too much on my plate to think about sleeping. I need to save the woman I love from an enemy. The same enemy that did this to my brother."

"Let us do that, sir," I say. "Stay here until Sean wakes up, and then you can join us."

He runs his hand through his hair. "I need to find her."

"I've found them, sir, and I know exactly how to get to them." Remington holds up the map.

"Sounds like you should trust your team. Being too close to the situation might make it worse." Ashe grips Rebel's shoulder.

"Maybe you're right, but if you don't have Fallon recovered by morning, I'll be coming for Nina."

CHAPTER 13

FALLON

"What is this place?" Maxim shoves me through the rusty door hanging from one hinge.

"I've already told you. Home," Nina snaps.

The sun is starting to break through the day, but the trailer is still dark inside. Nina yanks open the tattered curtains, and dust flies in the stale air.

"You don't live here." The dirty floor creaks, and I think I'm going to fall through it.

"This is where I grew up." She pulls open a door. "And this is where my hell began." I walk through, and there's a double bed with rotten-smelling, blood-stained sheets still on it. No headboard, just a frame. "And, that's where I slept." She points to a bare, torn-up twin mattress with a dingy yellow pillow on it.

"That was a step up from what I started with." She drags me by the hand to the fridge. She opens it, and the door of the old white box falls to the floor. It's empty. "This is how it always looked other than a few beer cans on the shelf."

A chill runs over me, not of fear, but of dread. "Did you bring me here to feel sorry for you that you had a shitty upbringing and that's why you're so evil?" I know in my gut this isn't the reason. I'm not sure I really want to know why.

She laughs and plops down on the brown plaid couch that has springs hanging out of the cushions. "You think we're a product of genetics or our upbringing?"

I look at a faded picture on the wall of a woman holding an infant, and a little girl is tucked by her side. Not your normal family picture. The mom is rail-thin and the little girl's hair is a mess, and her clothes are unkempt. A blanket obscures the face of the baby. "I think at some point, we chose the person we want to be, regardless of our upbringing," I finally answer her.

She pats the cushion next to her, and it lets out a moldy smell. "So, tell me sweet Fallon, if you were raised in this shithole, with a rotten corpse of your father, and a mother who was either drugged up, drunk, or had her legs spread wide for every man, and giving her daughter the same fate, you think you'd be as untarnished as you are?"

"I can see why it motivated you to want money, but you didn't have to do the things you've done to get it." I sit beside her, and Maxim hovers, watching us both closely.

"So, you think something good could've been grown from here? Men coming in and out at all hours of the night. Your own mother selling you to get her drugs. A child who had to steal for food and clothing?" Her eyes flicker with smothered emotions.

I look around the small room and picture the things she's saying. "I can't imagine a life like that."

She snickers. "Thanks to me, you never had to."

"I don't understand." That sinking feeling is back with a vengeance, and a wave of panic rolls over me.

She gets up and takes the picture off the wall. "Try this on for size. A little girl having to take care of a nameless little sister because her own parents didn't want her. I had to feed her, change her diapers, and take care of all her needs, and I couldn't even take care of myself. I was busy trying to steal food from dumpsters and putting my own mother back together every morning." She hands me the picture.

"What happened to her?" Nausea runs through me in waves.

"Some handsome fireman found her outside the station. That's the last I saw of her."

"So you saved your sister from your same fate?" Hot tears burn my eyes, threatening to take over.

"I grew up. I was very smart and got a scholarship to the best college. I learned all the ins and outs of genetic testing. I searched for my sister for years." She stands over me. "I finally found her."

God, please don't let it be. "I'm her," I whisper, and I can't stop my lip from shaking. "And I was with the man you betrayed." It's all starting to make sense now.

"The man I loved. The only man I've ever felt anything for."

My hand shakes with the picture grasped in it. "You said he loved me because I looked like you." My voice is as shaky as the rest of me, including my insides.

"That's right. See, I wasn't lying. He saw me in you. That's what attracted him to you."

"That's not true. We are nothing alike."

"And you have me to thank for that."

I stand. "You tried to kill me several times." The

realization of how dark-hearted she is rattles me even more.

She brushes a tendril of my hair off my shoulder. "You took my life, but as we've discussed before, if I wanted you dead, you'd already be in the ground."

"This is about getting back at me? You saved me from all of this just to torture me?" I lunge toward her and Maxim steps between us, holding me back.

She smiles a sickly smile. "Do you know I used to call you Cinderella? You know how the evil stepsisters felt about her." She walks around Maxim.

"I wasn't your stepsister."

"No, but you ended up with the handsome prince. How ironic."

"You don't really want Rebel. You just don't want me to have him."

"Now you're getting it. I knew you were a smart girl." She taps a finger to her temple.

"All this time. All the people you've hurt was to get back at me."

"That was only part of it, the rest I did for the sheer enjoyment of making money."

"You stole innocent young girls like Fiona and ruined their lives."

"I think if you checked the background of all the

alleged innocent girls, you'd find that their lives were nothing to begin with," she snickers.

"And you think you saved them?"

She shrugs one shoulder. "Maybe."

"You're more vile than I thought."

She rears back and slaps me across the face. "How dare you judge me after you've seen this place and what I did for you."

I hold my red-hot cheek. "That's just an excuse." I walk around the trailer. "I'm sure it was awful, and I'll forever be grateful that I didn't have to grow up feeling unloved or hungry, but there's no way I would've turned out like you. I chose who I wanted to be as an adult."

"You became your environment. You have no idea who you really are. Let me make it clear to you," she spits out in anger. "You're the daughter of a drug-dealing whore, who wanted nothing to do with the sight of you. Your so-called father never even held you in his arms. Born to two wretched, selfish people, and may I add, beyond worthless." She steps up close to me. "And, a sister that loved you enough to let you go and take the abuse that you would've received."

"Why didn't you stay with me that night at the fire station?"

"I didn't have a choice. I had to take care of them. Someone had to make them pay for their sins."

"Who's going to make you pay for yours, Nina?"

"The sin of saving you?" She huffs. "I think you owe me."

I reach out and touch her hand. "I'm sorry that your life was so horrible. No child should ever have to live like this. You should've been loved and cared for and cherished every day." I feel sorry for the child inside her that should've been adored.

She jerks her hand away, and I see glistening tears in her eyes threatening to rain down. "I don't want your fucking pity!" She storms out the door, and Maxim stands guard. I slowly walk around looking at every detail and grip the picture frame in my hand. I still can't believe the baby in this picture is me or that any of this is real. She lived in a nightmare that she saved me from. There has to be a way to save her back. She was never shown any love or kindness. It's no wonder she's a narcissistic monster. But...she's my sister. I have to try to help her regardless of what she's done to me.

I peek outside the curtain and see her pacing in the dirt, talking to herself. I'm sure she has an inward battle going on inside her. I open and close drawers, stopping when I find a photo album. The pictures are stuck under clear plastic sheets. They're old and yellowed, but they're of a young couple that appear to be in love. I peel back the plastic and take the picture out. It's dated before either one of us was born. "What happened to this happy couple that made them terrible parents?" I whisper to myself and tuck the picture into my back pocket, along with a school picture of Nina. She looks to be kindergarten age. I find one picture of me that looks like the day I was born here in this run-down trailer. I'm wrapped in a sheet, lying on my mother's belly. My father is next to her smoking a cigarette. Nina must've taken the picture. This is all so surreal. I feel like I'm living someone else's nightmare. Josie and I had such a happy childhood. We loved each other deeply, and poor Nina had no one. Not one person that loved her, until Rebel.

She storms back inside the trailer. "You have one last chance at freedom. I'll give you enough money to disappear for the rest of your life. All you have to do is promise never to see or talk to Derrick or his team again. Take someone with you if you have to. I'll never harm them or you. But if you break our deal, I'll kill every one of them."

"I thought part of the deal was that you'd turn yourself in?"

"That's off the table."

"So, you'll be free to continue trafficking young girls?"

"I'll stop. I'll keep all my business dealings legit. I give you my word."

"Your word means nothing to me."

"How about the word of your sister. I'll turn over a new slate."

"Why? Why should I believe you?"

"Because I don't want you to think of me as a monster." Sincerity fills her eyes, along with unshed tears.

No, she deserves to be punished for the things she's done. She doesn't get to walk away because I feel sorry for her. I'll make her think we have a deal. "Deposit the money in my account, and after that, I'll walk away." I stick out my hand.

"I knew you were like me. Money is far too enticing." The ungodly Nina is back with no signs of tears left. She shakes my hand, and my stomach rolls. "I'll have Maxim get cash. You need money available so that Derrick can't track you. I'll teach you how to disappear without a trace."

CHAPTER 14

THORN

"We're all set, Captain," I say, looking over the gear that Theo brought us.

"I'm counting on the four of you to bring Fallon back alive." He looks at each of us. Combined, we're a force to be reckoned with. "Thorn, you lead them. Mad Dog, you arm them with what they need. Remington, show them the way." He turns toward Theo. "You bring Hazel back unharmed." Rebel presses a finger into Theo's chest.

"I will, sir."

He pulls me aside. "This mission is no longer to bring Nina back alive. Do you understand me?"

"Yes, sir."

"Don't let harm come to any of these men," he

adds. "Keep me posted, and if you aren't back by the time Sean wakes up, I'll be joining you."

We all make our way to the rooftop to meet the military chopper landing to pick us up and take us to a remote area in Washington not far from Forks. We buckle in and devise a plan based on the map.

"As soon as we land, we should be able to make it on foot to this point in fifteen minutes. We'll have the advantage of the sun not rising for another thirty minutes. Theo, you'll line up here in the woods to take out any unwelcome visitors. Remington, you'll check for explosives and disarm them. Mad Dog, you'll take out the man that's been with Nina the entire step of the way. I'll protect Fallon and take out Nina. We'll back each other up."

They nod in agreement, and we ride in silence. This mission can't end soon enough. I want to get back and check on Lauryn. Who am I kidding? I can't wait to get back to see where things are headed between the two of us. She'll take some convincing to give us a chance, but I know she has feelings for me. It's written in her body language the few times we've been together. I've had my career as a SEAL; I need more now. I want a woman to come home to every night. Not just any woman, but Lauryn. I long to feel her legs wrapped around my body with nothing in between us. We can sneak around or get it out in the open. I'll leave the decision up to her, but I won't be going to bed alone again with her this close to me. This entire situation with Fallon and Rebel has made me realize I can have both a career and someone to love. I'm tired of being lonely.

I've been lost in my own thoughts so long that I'm taken off guard when the pilot says we're ready to land. We grab our gear, put on our vests, and load our weapons, having them ready to go. Orange streaks are on the horizon. "Daylight will be here soon. Let's get a move on it," I order, and our feet hit the ground running.

Remington leads the way through the woods and up the side of a mountain. He stops almost full run and hits the ground. We all follow suit. I crawl up next to him.

"There, just past the trees. Two men are standing guard at the entrance."

Six old, falling down trailers are scattered down a dirt road. A forgotten dumpster is sitting near the back of the so-called park, creating a stench.

"You used to live here?" I ask him, covering my nose.

"That one." He points to the one by the dumpster. "Dear old dad used to cook up his meth in the shed behind the trailer."

I pull my weapon from my belt. "Someday, you'll have to tell me all about it. For now, go scope it out for explosives." He crawls away mumbling something about his father blowing himself up.

Theo maneuvers next to me. "I can take these two jokers out easily."

"We need it to be done silently. If Nina's in there, we don't want to spook her and force her to do something stupid." I look over my shoulder at Mad Dog. "You stay close to me, while Theo takes care of them."

Theo takes out a small tin from his bag and smears black stripes on his face, then moves stealthily toward the guard. He sneaks up behind one, slitting his throat before the other knows what happened. The second one, Theo comes out of nowhere and the last thing I see is the guard's boots flying in the air.

The radio on my belt chirps. "Thorn. I found two different bombs set up. I'll start disarming them, but be careful. There may be more."

"Got it," I respond. "Theo, watch your step and keep an eye out for more men." I motion for Mad Dog to follow me. We get to our feet and work our way toward the trailer with guns high. We scatter behind a rusted-out abandoned car when the door of the trailer flies open. Nina paces up and down the length of the leaning mobile home, talking to herself.

"I can take her down," Theo radios.

"No. We don't know for sure that Fallon is inside, and if we kill her, we'll never find out where she's holding her."

"Roger that," Theo says.

A few minutes later, Nina goes back inside.

"I want complete silence. No shooting until absolutely necessary. We don't know how many men she has." Mad Dog nods, and the door opens again. It's the same large man that's been seen with Nina. He heads toward the SUV parked outside the trailer.

"Stop him," I order Mad Dog, and he takes off on foot. I make my way to the side of the trailer and slide quietly along the dirty wall. I hear Nina talking to someone inside. Just before I open the door, a honking noise comes from the SUV. Mad Dog and the guy are wrestling inside. "Damn it." I fling open the door, and Nina has her arm wrapped around Fallon's throat from behind, and a gun pointed at her head.

"Pretty boy back to save you." Nina smiles. "Drop it."

"Don't do it, Thorn. She's not going to hurt me," Fallon says.

"Don't count on it!" Nina snarls and presses her fingers deep into Fallon's neck, choking her.

"Let her go," I say, laying my weapon down. I don't want a repeat of last time with Fallon bleeding on the ground.

"Seems like a familiar sight. Derrick's always sending you in to save his girl." She looks around me. "Where is he?"

"Taking care of his brother you threw in the ocean."

"Poor Sean. I do hope he survives." She releases Fallon's throat but keeps the gun in place. Fallon bends over, gasping for air. "See, he loves his brother more than he does his fiancé. Otherwise, he'd be here," she hisses at Fallon.

"Don't listen to her bullshit." I lift my hands in the air. "If you let her go, you can walk out of here alive," I offer Nina.

"You didn't come here alone. As soon as your men see me, they'll kill me."

"I'll call them off, all you have to do is walk away." I inch toward them.

"Pretty boy thinks I'm stupid or that I didn't

predict their every move." She yanks Fallon's head back by the hair, and she winces.

"Please, Nina. You and I've already made a deal. These men don't have to die," Fallon chokes out.

Mad Dog storms through the door. "One down," he growls.

"You killed Maxim?" she yells and raises her gun in Mad Dog's direction and fires. It hits him in the chest, knocking him outside the door onto the ground.

An explosion goes off, and Remington comes running into the trailer. "We have to get out of here now! She's rigged this place to blow."

"Get out of my way," she snarls. She waves the gun for us to move to the back of the trailer. We do, and she walks with Fallon then pushes her in our direction, keeping the gun aimed at her.

"Derrick should've been the one to save her," she says. In slow motion, I see her move her finger to pull the trigger. I dive in front of Fallon, and she's screaming "she won't do it!" Her gun wavers at the last minute, and the bullet hits me square in the chest, knocking me to the floor. Nina runs out, and Fallon flies after her.

"Stop!" she screams.

I regain my breath and pull the bullet from my

vest. I get up and go after both of them, snagging my gun before I do. Theo has his aim on Nina, and she's frozen in place.

"Please don't kill her, Theo," Fallon begs and steps in front of her, holding her arms out to her side.

"Do it," Nina taunts.

I snatch the gun from Nina's grasp, and Theo steps closer.

"Please don't, Theo, I'm begging you," Fallon says.

"She deserves to die for the things she's done," Theo snarls.

"I know, you're right, she does, but she's my sister."

"What?" Theo cocks his head.

"It's true. She has the DNA reports to prove it."

"Just because she's blood doesn't make her your sister. That role was Josie's, and because of her, she's dead." Theo keeps his aim strong.

"Thorn, tell him not to kill her. She can live the rest of her days behind bars." She tugs on my arm.

"That didn't work out so well last time," Theo responds with anger.

"Guys, we have about ten seconds before this place goes up in flames," Remington interrupts.

A hissing noise starts from behind us. Mad Dog

grabs Nina's arm and starts running. Sparks start flying, and everyone runs for safety. Theo rushes to Fallon and tucks her protectively into him. He takes cover with her in the woods. I watch as each trailer one by one blows up into flames as bombs go off. Debris flies through the air and Theo covers Fallon's body with his. He stays over her until there are no more explosions. He rolls off and gets to his feet, helping her up.

I move from behind the SUV that's now on fire and head in their direction. "You okay?"

"Thanks to you. I can't believe she was really going to shoot me again." Fallon's expression is somber.

"I wasn't going to let that happen after the last hostage situation. Call it my redemption if you will." I get on my radio. "Mad Dog, do you have her?"

The radio hisses. "No."

"Where the fuck is she?" I want to crush the radio with my bare hands.

Remington walks up beside us. "I thought you were taking care of the bombs." Theo is in his face.

"I could only disarm one of them with the equipment I had on hand. The others were set to explode if the first one was disarmed, and then they triggered one another on a timer. She knew we were coming after her."

Through the smoke, Mad Dog storms in our direction, and I hear the sound of a bike revving. A few seconds later, Nina peels out from behind the dumpster on a dirt bike. Theo takes off after her on foot with Mad Dog on his heels. She races by them, shooting them a bird. Theo runs down the hill, trying to cut her off before she can make it down the mountain. She shoots between trees, and he barely misses her as he leaps toward her. He rolls a few feet before he can get to his feet and watches her disappears down the mountain. Theo and Mad Dog, with their heads hung down in defeat, dredge toward us.

I get on the horn with Rebel. "Sir, we lost Nina, but we have Fallon."

"Bring her home, and we'll regroup to find Nina." His voice is filled with relief and anger at the same time. "I'll have Honor send a car to your location for extraction."

Within thirty minutes, a military jeep is barreling toward us. Before it even comes to a complete stop, I open the passenger's side door. "You didn't happen to see anyone on a dirt bike?" I ask the driver, and he shakes his head.

I climb in the passenger side, and Theo tucks

Fallon in the backseat with him. "You okay?" I see Theo kiss her forehead in the side mirror.

"I don't know," she says. "I don't know if anything will ever be the same again." She lays her head on his shoulder, and her body starts to shake with tears.

"Let's get you home where you belong," he tells her.

We pull out, and I see her glance over her shoulder, looking at the still-burning trailers. The fire trucks arrive as we pull out of the dirt road.

She curls into Theo's side. "Is Sean going to be okay?"

"As good as can be expected. Rebel flew in a world-class neurosurgeon that Sean is friends with to operate on him. He did what he could, but he's deaf."

She lays her head on Theo's lap and cries. "I'm so sorry. This is all my fault."

"None of this is on you, Hazel." He holds her and lets her cry until exhaustion takes over and she falls asleep.

CHAPTER 15

REBEL

"How's Fallon?" I sit beside my brother's bed, holding his hand, talking to Thorn on the phone.

"Physically, she'll be okay. Nina told her about being her sister," he adds in a hushed voice.

"Let me talk to her."

"She just fell asleep, sir. I don't want to wake her. She's been through enough."

"How did Nina get away?" I want to yell but keep my voice low.

"Mad Dog grabbed her when the explosions started. He got hit by flying debris, and it knocked him down. When he got to his feet, she was gone. She took off on a dirt bike."

I get up and walk into the hallway. "Why is she

still alive? You should've killed her the minute you laid eyes on her?"

"Because Fallon begged us not to, sir."

"This will never be over until she's dead." I run my hand through my hair. "Get back here, and we'll go after her again."

"How's your brother?" he asks after a long moment.

I look back into Sean's room. "He hasn't woken up yet."

"We're getting on a plane shortly. Do you want us to take Fallon to headquarters?"

"No. Bring her to me. She'll want to see Sean."

"Yes, sir."

* * *

Fallon runs into my arms when she sees me outside Sean's room. "Thank god, you're okay." I place my hands on either side of her bruised-up face and softly kiss her lips. Her arms tuck around my waist, and she holds me tight.

"I thought I'd never see any of you again."

"I'd never let that happen." I kiss her face repeatedly.

"Is Sean awake?" She looks up through her tears.

"Not yet. He stirred a little bit but nothing yet." I see Ashe heading down the long hallway, stopping when he reaches me.

"This must be Fallon." He smiles at her. "Do you want me to examine her?" he asks me.

"How about you check out Sean first. I'm not ready to let her go." I tuck her into my side, where she belongs.

We walk into Sean's room, and he pulls out a penlight and starts his examination. He shakes Sean's shoulder, and his eyes blink open.

"Where am I?" His voice is barely above a rasp.

Ashe picks up a whiteboard beside his bed and starts scribbling on it, then shows it to Sean.

"Why is no one talking?" he asks and tries to sit up when he sees Fallon. "You're okay," he says.

She sits on the side of his bed and takes the board from Ashe and writes him a message. I see the word deaf on the board. Sean's body starts to tremble as he reads the words she's written. Fallon crawls in bed with him and holds him.

Ashe places his hand on my shoulder and walks me into the hallway. "He'll be okay. There are things that can be done to help him adapt. With some therapy, he'll get use back in his leg, but it's going to take some time. He's alive and in one piece. That's what matters."

"Thanks for everything you've done for him," I say.

"I'll stick around until tomorrow just to make sure nothing else pops up unexpectedly, then I need to get home to my beautiful wife."

"You finally talked her into marrying you, huh?"

He chuckles. "I still can't believe it myself. I'm one lucky man after everything I put her through." He slaps me on the back. "My advice to you is to put a ring on that lady's finger before she figures out what a pain in the ass you are."

"I couldn't agree more," I snort. "I'll let things get back to normal first."

"I'm not sure the word normal is in the vocabulary of men like us." He laughs.

Thorn's large body fills the hallway as he heads in my direction.

"I'll check on him later." Ashe shakes my hand before he leaves.

"Sir, we're headed back to headquarters for debriefing."

"It can wait until tomorrow. I want all of you to get some rest first." I sniff the air. "And maybe a shower."

Thorn smells his armpit. "Priorities," he says. "I wanted you to know that all the local airfields and ports are shut down in Washington. Nina's picture is plastered all over the news, and the police departments have been notified. The coast guard is on high alert too."

"None of that will stop her. She's too damn smart and good at her own game."

"I'll see you back at headquarters." He marches back the same way he came in the hospital.

Sean's hand is shaking as he writes something to Fallon on the whiteboard. She reads it and quickly erases it. "I think we should go and let him rest," she says, climbing out of his bed. She leans down and kisses his cheek.

I walk over and take the board and write that I'll be back in the morning to see him. He nods and places the board on his lap.

I take Fallon's hand and lead her to my truck, opening the door for her to get inside. She doesn't scoot to the middle like she normally does. Instead, she rests her head on the window.

I back out of the parking lot and head home. "You okay?"

She indicates yes with her head.

"Do you want to talk about it?"

"Not really." She lies down, placing her head in my lap.

"I'm so sorry about everything that's happened to you. I want nothing more than to keep you safe."

"She's my sister," she whispers, and I feel her tears soak through my pants.

"I know. Tate found a journal with a letter inside."

She sits up. "Where's the journal?"

"Locked in the safe in my office."

"I want to read it."

"Okay, but it can wait until tomorrow. I want to get you home and hold you."

She lays her head back down and doesn't speak for the rest of the ride. We take the elevator to our apartment, and as soon as we're in the door, I hold her against me. "How about a hot shower and something to eat?"

"I'm not hungry, but a shower sounds good."

I lead her to the bathroom and strip her out of her clothes.

"Wait," she says, picking her pants up off the floor. She pulls pictures out of her back pocket and lays them face down on the counter. "We can talk about it later," she says, pressing her lips to mine. We step into the shower with our hands all over one another. She winces when I touch her side.

"Sorry, baby." I kneel down and place soft kisses on her wounds.

"It's okay, don't stop," she rasps and runs her hands through my hair.

I gently and slowly make love to her. It's hard to control myself, thinking that I was so close to losing her forever. I want to make her feel safe and loved in my arms. After I've touched every inch of her body, I lift her up and slide into her warmth. She moans and gives into me. I barely move inside her. I want to keep her right where she is as long as I can. We find our release together as the water starts to lose its heat.

I quickly wash her body and get out, wrapping her snuggly in a towel. I dry her hair and brush it out. Her eyes look heavy, and her body looks exhausted. I pick her up and carry her to bed, crawling in next to her.

"I love you, Fallon. I don't know what I'd do without you," I say, tucking her back into my chest.

"I love you, too," she whispers as she drifts off to sleep safely in my arms.

* * *

When I wake up the next morning, the bed next to me is empty. "Fallon?" I slide into a pair of jeans and go looking for her. She's not in the apartment. "Damn it," I mutter and pull on a T-shirt, heading downstairs barefooted. "Have you seen Fallon?" I ask Honor, who's sitting at her desk with a cup of coffee, and Lawson is in the chair across from her.

"Hey, man. Glad everyone made it home safe," he says as he stands.

"Fallon. Have you seen her?" I ask again.

"She's in the war room," Honor says.

I pad down the hall and see her through the large window, talking on the phone. I stop in the doorway and listen.

"I need as much information as you can find on Nina's personal life. If you find any living relatives, I need to see them." She hangs up the phone, looking more lost than the first day I met her.

"Do you think that's a good idea?" I ask, taking the seat next to her. I'm assuming she was talking to someone from the FBI.

"I know Nina gave me the highlights of my real parents, but there has to be more to the story, and I need to find Nina. She and I have some unfinished business that needs to be handled."

I lean my elbows on the table. "Business about your family?"

She bites the inside of her cheek. "Yes. I need to know more."

My gut tells me she's hiding something. "I understand your need to learn more, but you can't trust her to tell you the truth."

"May I have her journal?"

"Yes, but I was hoping you'd take some time to recover first."

"I need answers, not time," she snaps and stands abruptly.

"Will you let me help you through this?"

She lays her hand on my cheek. "I love you, but I want to work through this on my own. I need to make sure there's nothing else she can hurt us with again."

"We'll find her, and she'll be locked away for life this time."

"When she is, I want to see her."

"I don't want you anywhere near her ever again." I join her on my feet.

"She's my sister." She presses her lips together as if she's choosing her words.

"She had a piece of paper with DNA results.

They could've been anyone's. We both know she's capable of fabricating anything she wants to."

"I do, but I know she's telling the truth. The timeline adds up. The only thing my parents told me was that I was found abandoned at a firehouse." She turns her body toward me to look me in the eye. "You know it's true too. Think about it. We have the same features and coloring. You've said so yourself." She glances down, and I lift her chin.

"That's not what attracted me to you, and you know it. I hated her. If you reminded me of her, I wouldn't have fallen in love with you."

"You fell in love with me over time. At first, you wanted nothing to do with me."

"I wanted nothing to do with women or love." I kiss her lips. "But you saved me. You mended my broken heart and filled it with love for only you."

She sits and leans back in her chair. "I don't know who I am anymore." A tear slides down her cheek.

"You're the same person you've always been. Sweet, loving, tough as nails, Fallon."

She looks away, not wanting to believe me.

"You need time to process everything you've been through. I don't want to leave you alone today, but I have to go by the hospital this morning and meet with Ashe. He's making one last assessment of Sean, and I want to know when I can bring him home."

"Okay, I want to be there too."

"I'd like to see you eat something first. You've lost weight."

"I don't have an appetite after the things I've seen."

"I'm bringing in a temporary team psychiatrist while Dr. Ruth does some healing of her own. I'd really like for you to see him."

"I will, I promise, but not today."

CHAPTER 16

THORN

I open the door to my apartment quietly in case Lauryn is still sleeping. I'm caught off guard when she's sitting on the couch, sipping a cup of coffee, wearing one of my SEAL T-shirts.

"You feeling better?" I ask while emptying my pockets.

"Sore, but better." She watches my every move.

I push the coffee table out of the way and kneel down in front of her. I pick up her empty hand and inspect the bruises on her wrists. "I'm sorry she hurt you because of me."

She places her mug on the side table and rests her hand on my cheek. "It wasn't your fault."

"She knew about us, about everything." I look back and forth into her eyes.

"She's good and knows her victim's Achilles' heel."

"That's a good way to describe how I feel about you." I lean in and kiss her softly, even though my tendency is to devour her.

When she pulls back, she presses her forehead to mine with her eyes closed. "I've thought about you for years," she whispers as she reaches down and places her mug on the floor.

I don't need another opening from her. I sweep her into my arms and carry her to my bed. Placing her on her feet, neither one of us wastes time removing our clothes. When she's naked, my gaze sweeps over her sexy body—the body of a woman, not the young girl I remember. Her neck and collarbone long to be kissed by me. Her breasts are the perfect size, and her nipples are tight, asking to be in my mouth. The curve of her waist is sexy and leads to her bare mound. Scanning further, her long, lean legs are silky and firm. My cock stands at attention, picturing her legs around my waist.

"You're more beautiful than I remember." I slip my hands around her core.

"Make love to me," she says, staring into my eyes.

"I'm not the same boy from years ago," I tell her

while lying her on the bed. "I like to be in control," I add.

"I'm okay with that." She blinks her long, dark lashes.

I open the bedside drawer, taking out a condom and rolling it on, then start at her feet, working my way up her body with my hands. Then my lips follow the path I created back down her body. "Roll over," I command, and she does. I grab her hips and pull them up, and I lean my body into her so that she can feel how hard she makes me.

She groans and arches her back. I slide my hands to her breast and twist lightly at her nipples, and she mewls, pressing her ass into me.

I lift one hand and smack her ass. She looks over her shoulder with lust-filled eyes. "Do it again." She licks her lips.

Who am I to not give a woman what she wants? Part of my control is meeting her needs. I smack her other cheek a little harder this time, leaving my hand-print on her. Then I rub her drenched center, giving her nothing but pleasure. As I push my fingers into her, I stroke my cock. "You're fucking sexy," I groan.

She lies flat on her belly then rolls over, planting one long leg around my ass. Her eyes grow large as she watches my hand move up and down my length.

I nearly come in my hand when she licks her full lips. "I want to feel you inside of me." She pants out her words.

She replaces my hand with hers, and I inch toward her entrance. I move down, placing one hand behind her. "Arms above your head," I say between gritted teeth.

She smiles and does as she's told, grasping the headboard. I lower my head and draw a nipple into my mouth. One of her hands flies off the headboard and wraps around my neck.

I stop sucking but don't take my lips from around her nipple. "Put your hand back," I command.

She does and pushes her back up, pressing further into my mouth. I chuckle. "You're not very good at being submissive."

"I'm sorry. I'll try harder next time, but you're driving me crazy," she says between pants of breath.

I lean back on my knees and wrap her other leg around my waist, and dive deep inside her. I have to bite my lip hard to keep control. Her warmth floods over me, and I crave her even more. I don't move, and I can already feel her insides starting to pulsate around my cock.

"Breathe, baby," I say, and she slows her breaths. Once she's gained her control, I rock back and forth inside her, leisurely at first. Her lips part and she's gasping again. I move all the way out and plunge in again, deeper this time. "Play with your nipples," I order.

She releases the headboard and sexy as shit, runs her hands slowly down to her breast, squeezing them first. My cock throbs with the sight of her. Her bottom lip is gripped between her teeth as a moan escapes. Her fingers toy with her taut nipples, twisting, letting go, then repeating.

My balls draw up and start to tingle, forcing me to thrust harder. I slide my hand between us and tweak her nub. Her body vibrates as she lets pleasure overtake her senses. She squeezes me tight, drawing me deeper inside her as she comes. The sensation is earth-shattering, and I can't stop my body's reaction to her. I growl with my release as my muscles start to shake. I cover her body with my body and trap her mouth with mine, swallowing both our cries of satisfaction. When our bodies are spent, I lie next to her, caressing her soft skin.

"I didn't hurt you, did I?"

She rolls up on to her side with her elbow propping her up. "Not in the least."

I lift her hand and kiss the bruises encompassing her wrists. "When these heal, I'll be the one tying you up, and I won't leave bruises unless you resist too much."

She smiles broadly. "You aren't the same lover I recall, and I don't want to know how and why you changed. I'll let that be privileged information."

I laugh. "Good because I've lots of new skills I'd like to share with you." I move off the bed and toss the condom in the wastebasket and pull on a pair of jeans.

She draws the sheet up under her chin. "Where are you going?"

I walk over to the foot of the bed and yank the sheet off, exposing her. "I've got a debriefing downstairs, and we've got to map out a plan to find Nina."

She gets out of bed and finds her clothes on the floor. "You didn't bring her back?"

"No. She got away when the place exploded."

"I can help. I studied her whenever she was around."

"You're not going anywhere near the action, but there is a journal that was Nina's. It's from her childhood. I'm sure it will give you more insight as to her inner workings."

"Where is it?" She tucks my shirt into her slacks.

"Rebel has it, but there is something you should know."

"What?"

"Nina claims that Fallon is her long-lost sister."

"Seriously?" Her eyes grow wide.

"She has DNA proof."

"Damn. How is Fallon taking the news?"

"She begged us not to kill Nina."

"She's got to feel lost, given this information." She heads toward the door.

"Even though I think you should take some time off, Fallon could use your help right now." I push the door shut when she opens it. "You and I need to figure out our situation."

She turns and leans against the door. "I...we... should let things settle down. We both got carried away." She glances toward the bedroom.

"No. What we did was bound to happen sooner or later. I told you things weren't done between us and they still aren't."

"We could both lose our jobs."

"I don't give a shit. I'll step down." I stare into her eyes, so she knows I'm dead serious.

She places her hand on my cheek. "We'll find another way, but for now, I need to focus on helping our team."

"I agree. Just don't shut down on me now that we've found each other again."

"Okay," she whispers against my lips.

"Unless you want everyone to know we're together, I suggest you go change your clothes. I'll head down to the war room."

She glances down at my T-shirt she's wearing. "That's probably a good idea."

"You can wear my clothes anytime you want. Better yet, nothing at all would be preferable."

"I'll make note of it." She giggles and heads out the door in the opposite direction from me.

I take the stairs two at a time to find Rebel in his office on the phone.

"I know she escaped! You don't have to remind me!" He's all but yelling into the phone. "No, sir, the mission isn't over." He listens for a moment with his jaw clenched.

"Yes, Commander." He slams down the phone. "Fuck!"

"He's not letting us go after Nina." I grip the back of the leather chair.

"No. He wants to let things around her die down and watch for her to rebuild."

"By then, there is no telling how many more girls will go missing!" I throw my hands in the air. I hear a noise behind me and turn to see Fallon walk into the office.

"We have to find her," she says, walking over to Rebel.

"It's no longer our mission. Commander Lukas is redirecting our efforts to another project that's developing overseas. He'll be here tomorrow with another team to brief us. We leave next week."

"No. I won't let Nina start again!" She goes to walk away, and Rebel grasps her arm.

"You can't stop her. We can't even locate her. Besides, we have a short window of time."

"Time for what? What are you talking about?"

Rebel gets down on one knee. "To get married. We postponed it before, and I swore if you made it back alive, I wouldn't go another day without making you my wife."

Fallon's demeanor softens when she sees the larger than life Rebel gets down on one knee. Slowly, she joins him on the ground. "I thought the same thing many times. Every mission you go on could be your last, and that scares the hell out of me. But I love you, and I don't want to waste any more time either." He snatches her to him and kisses her, and it's my cue to step out and shut the door behind me.

I run into Theo on my way out. "Is Rebel in his office?" He points past me to the door.

"Yeah, but he's a little busy at the moment."

"Busy or not, we need to get back out there and find Nina."

I grab his shoulder before he can open the door. "It's not our mission anymore. Commander Lukas is sending us with another team overseas."

"I'm not going anywhere until Nina is behind bars. She won't stop, and more girls will be at risk. I'm not letting her put another woman through what she's done to Fiona!" he yells.

"We don't have another option right now," Rebel says as he comes out of his office with Fallon tucked to his side.

"You have to convince him to go after her." Theo stands up to Rebel.

"I want her captured more than anyone, but we've been ordered to stand down for now. So unless you want to resign, you'll do your job." He's firm with Theo. "She'll resurface, and we'll go after her."

Theo lets out a long, deep sigh. "What's this mission?"

He claps Theo's shoulder. "We'll be briefed tomorrow. Today's mission is to marry this beautiful woman." He kisses the top of Fallon's head.

"Today?" she asks. "We can't get married until Sean is out of the hospital."

"Agreed. I'm headed there now to see if he can

come home. If not today, then this week at the latest. I'm not going anywhere until we have rings on our fingers." He smacks her ass and walks out.

"Congratulations," I say.

Fallon steps up to Theo. "Would you be my best man?"

"I'd be honored." He hugs her.

I take a step to walk away. "And, Thorn, I need someone to walk me down the aisle."

"You're asking me?" I raise an eyebrow.

"You've saved my life twice now. You're protective like a father would be." She casts her eyes downward.

"I'd be honored to." I crook a finger under her chin and lift it, and she smiles.

"Thank you, both."

CHAPTER 17

NINA

"Damn them all to hell!" I watch from an abandoned building across the road as Fallon catches up with Derrick, and they drive off together.

"I guess she decided not to hold up her end of our agreement," I talk to myself. "I'll have to remind her of what I'm capable of doing." I sit on the cold concrete floor and place the binoculars next to me.

"Why, Derrick, of all people did you have to fall for my sister?" I answer my own ramblings. Because she's sweeter, prettier, younger, and way more innocent than I am. But, she's not smarter or wealthier, not that those things seem to matter to him. I can be sweet. Can't I? If I'd have been given the life she had, maybe.

It goes back to my question, nature or nurture? I

could walk away from my nature and have a different life, couldn't I? Or would I always go back to being me? I'd be like her if it meant Derrick would love me. It would be rather boring, and I'd more than likely lose interest, but I could do it for a man like him.

It's my fault she won him in the first place. If I would've worked harder for him to be removed from his mission, he wouldn't have found out that I was the one that betrayed him. He'd be none the wiser as to my extracurricular activities.

"Why can't I let him go?" I should be a million miles away right now, never to be found, and here I sit, only a few hundred feet from the men who've been hunting me. Is it merely for him, or some sick, gnawing feeling to be around my sister? Why didn't I kill her when I had the chance?

Because like it or not, she's all the family you have left. It wasn't her fault that she wasn't around. She's the lucky one. She could've let them kill me, but she didn't. She begged them. I need to give her life beyond Derrick. She's not the kind of woman that will support his lifestyle for long. She may think she loves him, but the danger he and his men live in will grow weary on a girl like her. She deserves better. I guess it's up to me again to keep her safe.

"Look at me, the big sister always doing what's

best for her family." I laugh. And Derrick thinks I'm all bad. I'll send her away and keep him for myself. He'll need comforting knowing the woman he supposedly loves left him. He'll drown his sorrows in liquor again, and I'll be the one to pick up the pieces. He'll lose his SEAL status and want to disappear right into my waiting arms.

I'll make her nothing more than a distant memory for him. I can make him happy. I'll even adopt a few bratty kids if that's what he wants. I have plenty of money to hire a nanny to care for them, so they don't get in my way.

"I have just the plan for you, Fallon Davis, never to be Mrs. Derrick Rebel." I tuck my hair under my cap and sneak out of the building and head for Fallon's office. It's locked up tight but no match for my skills. I break in, sight unseen, and make my way up the stairs. I jimmy her door open and see her bloodstains on the floor from the last time I was here. I sit in her chair and rock back.

"This is what it feels like to be my sister." Rather boring. I open a drawer and take out pen and paper, putting my design into motion. When I'm done with her, Derrick will never see her again or want her back. I'll pick the perfect moment to execute my plan.

I finish the letter and head to the store, purchasing three burner phones, purple hair dye, and a frumpy dress I'd never be caught dead in. I hand the cashier a trumped-up credit card and take out some cash.

Once I've checked into a hotel, I chop off my long hair and dye it. It's hideous, but they won't be looking for a woman with purple hair. I don the ugly dress and head to the streets of Portland. I take out a wad of cash when I see a homeless man on the street.

"How would you like to make a few hundred bucks?" I ask the man whose clothes are barely hanging on his thin frame.

He smiles and has two teeth missing in the front. "What do I have to do, lady?"

"Come with me. I'll show you who I need you to deliver a gift to. Easy peasy. I'll even feed you."

He willingly follows me.

CHAPTER 18

REBEL

Ashe is in Sean's room when we arrive at the hospital. "What do you think, Doc. Can he come home today?"

"What did you say?" Sean squints at me and tugs at his ear. Fallon picks up the board and starts writing.

"I think you should give him more time. He's going to need to go to short-term therapy," Ashe tells me.

"He can do that at my place. I'll have everything he needs. I have the perfect person to get his ass moving." Lawson already volunteered to help him.

Ashe drags me off to the side. "He's going to need a therapist too. He's been through a lot of trauma, and not being able to hear will only make it worse on him."

"I understand. I'll set up whatever he needs. Fallon can help teach him sign language. She has hearing issues and learned the language so that she could help people worse off than her. It will help that Sean adores her."

He looks over at them, and Fallon is already trying to teach him a few words. "I can see that." He turns toward me. "You don't need me anymore, and I'll be catching the next plane home."

I stick out my hand. "Thank you for saving him."

"I'm glad you called me. Anything you need, let me know."

"Tell your wife hello."

He smiles. "I still can't get used to calling her my wife, but god I love it."

"Marriage looks good on you, Ashe."

"When are you getting her down the aisle?" He glances over his shoulder at Fallon.

"As soon as Sean is home. Do you want to stick around for the wedding?"

"Thanks, but I'm headed home to my wife. Good luck, and congratulations." He slaps me on the back and tells Sean goodbye.

"He looks good," Sean says loudly.

"He does. Aedon finally got him under control."

"When can I go home?" Sean asks.

I hold up one finger. "One day." I take the board from Fallon and write on it, then turn it toward him.

The first smile I've seen in a while covers his face. "You two are finally getting married?"

I nod and add the word tomorrow on it, and that I need him to be my best man.

"I won't be able to walk." He looks down his body to his legs.

I'll wheel you down, I write. I'm not waiting another day, and I'm not having my brother miss the one, and only time I'm getting married, I add.

"I'm happy for both of you," he says, but his eyes grow sad.

What is it? Fallon writes.

"I'm messed up. I'll never find a woman now, and on top of it, I'll have to give up the bar."

Fallon writes quickly. *Any woman would be lucky to have a man like you. As far as the bar goes, you can hire someone to tend bar. You can enjoy being the owner rather than working all the time.*

"I enjoy tending bar."

I take the whiteboard from her. *Let's take it one day at a time. You'll figure it out and be back doing the things you love in no time,* I write.

"Like hearing? I rather enjoyed that," he says sarcastically.

"I'm sorry you got caught up in my mess and that you paid the price," I jot down and say the words out loud. I wish he could hear the words and the sincerity behind them. I should've done a better job of protecting all the people I care about. I've underestimated Nina every single time. I'm thankful that we got our people back safe, but I'm not sure any of them will ever be the same. Most especially, Fallon.

"I'm tired. You two need to get out of here and plan a wedding." Sean scoots down in the bed.

Fallon places a kiss on his cheek, and I pat his shoulder. "Tomorrow."

Fallon holds my hand as we walk down the hallway. "I feel so guilty that Nina involved him. It's my fault he lost his hearing."

"It's Nina's fault, not yours." She squeezes my hand.

"How about we head back home, and I make love to my fiancé one last time because the next time, I'll be making love to my wife."

"I'd like that." She wraps her arm around my waist.

"I've got a few fires to put out first, then I'm all yours." I kiss the side of her head.

"How is Dr. Ruth?" she asks.

"She's tough. She'll be fine, but I need to deal with Thorn."

"You mean him having the hots for Lauryn?" I raise a brow.

"How did you know about that?" I raise a brow.

"Have you not seen the way he lights up when she's in the same room with him?" she snorts.

"I guess I missed it. I've been a little preoccupied."

"Have you missed Lawson and Honor, too?" She laughs harder this time.

I stop dead in my tracks. "I guess I've missed a lot of things lately, and that has to stop. I'll have to lay down the law with all of them. No fraternizing."

"Really? Would that have stopped you?" She narrows her gaze at me.

"I guess they'll all be sneaking around. That's what I would do." I chuckle.

"I think if any one of them are lucky enough to find someone they love and accept the job they do, then more power to them. They deserve to have both."

"You are one smart lady." I draw her in closer to my side.

"Yes I am, and don't you forget it."

"Yes, ma'am," I tease.

* * *

When I get back, my team is gathered in the conference room. Theo stands when he sees me.

"I think we should talk to Commander Lukas and convince him to let us continue to chase Nina." His tone is firm.

I lean my hands on the table. "I think we need to step back. We've been chasing her for years now. We get close, but can't keep her. She's involved all of us now, and we're too close to the situation. A break from her might help."

"We're just supposed to walk away and let her ruin more innocent lives?" Theo's anger rises in his voice.

"No. The military will still be keeping tabs on her, and when she shows up again, a team will go after her. It just might not be us. Be thankful we all got out of it alive. It could've ended very differently."

He sits, crossing his arms over his chest, rage permeating from him.

"I know we all want Nina taken out of commission, but there are other evils to track down. She's only one in a large pond of players. We've lost focus on the bigger mission. It's our job to protect this country and keep its people safe. Nina is only a small part of that. Let's go after the ones we can. Nina's day will come eventually." Groans are heard around the room. "To the matter at hand before Commander Lukas gets here to set us up for the next project. It has come to my attention that there has been some fraternizing amongst us." Lawson looks down, and Thorn glares at me.

"Even though it's against policy, I'm not going to report it. I'm asking that you keep it out of the workplace and don't let it interfere with your jobs. If either one of those things happens, I will end it. Is that clear?"

Thorn gives a slight nod, and Lawson grins. "Yes, sir."

"Good. Now, I expect all of you to get some rest and be at my wedding tomorrow."

"Where is it going to be?" Tate asks.

"Sean's bar. It's been cleaned up, and he's coming home tomorrow. He'll be staying at headquarters with us until he's on his feet."

"I'm glad he's coming home," Theo responds. "I know Fiona would be glad to help him."

"Thanks. Fallon is going to teach him sign

language. Maybe they can tag team him to keep him busy."

"I'll mention it to her," he says.

"Okay, get out of here. We'll meet in the morning, and then I'll see you at the wedding."

They all scatter.

CHAPTER 19

FALLON

I can't believe it's finally happening. I'm marrying Rebel. It's been such a long time coming. I wish Josie were here to see it.

"You look gorgeous." Theo's voice pulls me out of my thoughts. "Rebel's going to die when he sees you in this dress." He holds my hand, and I twirl around in a circle for him to see.

"I'm glad I didn't return it. It's a little big on me now, but I didn't have time to have it taken in."

"You're perfect, and Rebel is one lucky man."

"So are you. I'm glad you have Fiona."

"Me too, but I'm wishing she was ready to take the next step."

"She's come so far, I'm sure she will soon."

"I don't know." He sits in the chair in his old apartment upstairs at Sean's place where I'm getting ready.

"Why do you say that?"

"She still won't...you know..."

I laugh at this tough guy's innocence. "You two still haven't had sex?"

"No. We've come close, but she always pulls back at the last minute."

"I know it's hard, no pun intended, but give her more time if that's what she needs. She's been through more than any of us can relate to."

"I don't plan on going anywhere. I'll wait forever if I have to."

"She's the lucky one." I ruffle my hand through his hair. "You're a good man, and she loves you."

He stands. "Are you ready for this?" He holds out his arm.

"It's not time, and I have one thing I need to do first."

"Do you need help?"

"No, it's something I need to do alone."

"You're not leaving the building, are you?"

"I'd love to go to Josie's gravesite, but Rebel would lose his mind if I were to go anywhere." I pull her favorite book out of my bag. "I just want some time alone with my thoughts."

"That I can do." He glances at his watch. "I'll come back for you in thirty minutes."

"Thorn's supposed to walk me down the aisle."

"He will, but I'm the best man, and I want to be the one on your arm when you walk downstairs."

"Okay." I kiss his cheek. "I love you, Theo."

"Back at you, Hazel." He slips away, and I curl up on the couch with Josie's book.

"I wish you could be here today. I wish so many different things for you. I miss you every day. You would love Rebel. He's fiercely protective yet loving. He's the strongest man that I know, yet gentle when it comes to me. He's tough on his men, but somehow melts in my arms."

A knock on the door interrupts me. I get up and open the door without looking. A man in dirty, tattered clothes hands me a box.

"A wedding gift," he says, and I take it from him.

"Who is it from?"

"A pretty rich lady," he says, and then runs down the stairs.

My heart picks up its pace as I place it on the coffee table. I slowly open the lid, and there is a phone and a letter inside. The envelope says: To my sister.

I peel it open and sit back to read it.

"Dearest Sweet Fallon,

I see that you didn't hold up your end of the deal. But, being the forgiving sister that I am, and I'm only looking out for your safety, I'm willing to give you one more chance.

Walk away. Disappear like I told you to, and I'll make sure this wedding doesn't end in Derrick's death. You can only take one person with you...anyone but Derrick. Maybe it will be that cute little soldier with the mechanical arm, Theo. Or, the strapping hero that saved your life when I shot you. Or, just maybe it will be that poor innocent girl whose life you claimed I stole.

Whoever you chose, I promise to never lay a hand on them or have my men harm them. It's that simple. I've deposited monies into an untraceable account for you, and I've left you directions on how to disappear without a trace.

If you ever contact Derrick or any of his men, all

bets are off. I'll kill him and his team one by one and leave you with the guilt of their deaths.

This is the second time I'm saving you from a life that will do nothing but cause you harm. Take it and say thank you, sister.

Your loving older sister,

Nina

The phone vibrates in the box. My hand trembles as I answer it.

"What's it going to be? Do I start the fireworks, or are you choosing wisely little sister?"

"You're fucking evil."

"That may be, but the clock is ticking."

"What about you? Are you going back into business?"

"Consider me retired if you disappear. I'll be keeping tabs on you. I'll know your every move, so as long as you follow the rules, I'll keep on the straight and narrow."

"I don't trust you," I snarl.

"You don't have any other choice. You have ten minutes to leave the building. If I don't see you getting in the car I left out back and heading out, I'll set the timer, and none of you will ever walk out. Your choice. Tick tock," she says, and hangs up.

I pack my bag and find the only person that makes sense to take with me. I can't give him a choice. There's not enough time. I open Sean's door to his apartment, and he's alone. He smiles when he sees me and stands with his cane.

I open the letter from Nina and hold it in front of him. He quickly reads it and understands why I'm here. Without question, I brace my side knowing it's going to hurt to help him up. I take his arm as he leans on me hard dragging his let, I lead him down the back way without being noticed. We climb into the car where a driver is waiting on us. As soon as he pulls out, the phone vibrates again.

"Good decision, and I agree with taking Sean. He's lost enough, and I don't have it in me to kill him."

"You better keep your word and not harm any of them."

"I don't want to kill the man that will eventually come running back to me." She laughs, and I hear silence on the other end of the phone.

The driver takes us to a private airport where a plane is waiting on us to board. I help Sean up the steps and into a plush seat. I stare out the window as tears fill my eyes when the plane takes its flight to our unknown destiny and a new life without the man I love.

Sean holds my hand and lets me cry.

CHAPTER 20

REBEL

"Where the hell is Sean?" I slam his apartment door. Maybe one of my men helped him down the stairs. I take them several at a time and look around the bar, not seeing him.

"Hey, it's time," Thorn says.

"I can't find my brother."

"I'll look for him," Lawson says.

"I'm going to go get your bride." Thorn turns to walk away, and Theo comes running up. "She's gone," he says breathlessly.

"Who's gone?"

"Fallon."

"What do you mean she's gone?"

"I can't find her anywhere. Her bags are even gone."

"Sean's missing too. You don't think Nina got to them?" Panic fills my chest.

"There is no way Nina got inside this building," Thorn chimes in but glances around the room.

"Fuck!" I try Fallon's phone. It rings then goes to voicemail. "Where are you? Call me! This can't be happening." I run outside and look around for her.

"Sir, I found this where you were to be standing to get married." Mad Dog hands me a phone. I dial the one phone number programmed into it. I know it's her.

"She finally wised up and left you." Nina laughs. "I knew she wasn't the right woman for you."

"What the fuck have you done to her?" I white knuckle the phone.

"I simply gave her a choice, and she didn't pick you."

"Make no mistake, I will find you and kill you without any reservations."

"If you kill me, you'll never find her or your brother." She laughs again. "What a sneaky girl. You only thought she was innocent. This entire time she's had a thing for your brother. I told her she could save one person in her life and she chose Sean, not her fiancé. Poor Derrick, betrayed again," she tisks.

"You better not harm either one of them." I grit my teeth.

"You're the only one that can keep them both safe. Come away with me."

"I fucking hate you. I'd never go anywhere with you except to your funeral to make sure that you were really dead."

"Oh, such hateful words to the woman that holds your balls in her hands."

"Where are they, Nina?" I yell.

"Gone, gone, gone, gone, gone. That's all I'll ever say about it."

"I will strangle you with my bare hands."

"Ah, I like it rough," she purrs.

"You are one sick bitch!"

"Now that's no way to talk to your future bride. We could make it happen today. You do already have a wedding planned and a missing bride. I've never seen you look so handsome in a suit."

"I'm done playing your games. I will hunt you down with or without my men. I will risk anything and everything to find you, and when I do, I'll show no mercy." I look outside the window for her. She can obviously see me.

"I love a good chase. In the meantime, while you're looking for me, remember Fallon will be living it up with your brother. I've got a plane to catch, handsome. Call me anytime." The line goes dead.

I go to my knees and scream at the top of my lungs. My team surrounds me. "I don't care what it takes, I'm going after her." I stand and rip off my jacket and throw it on the ground as I stand.

"We'll all go with you." Theo is on my heels, following me to my car.

"No. I'm done being a SEAL. I've played by the rules, and it's gotten me nowhere. I need to play as dirty as she does, and I can't do that leading this team."

"That's what she wants, Derrick." Lauryn steps up beside me. "She wants to ruin everything you've worked for all these years. If she takes everything away from you, she thinks you'll have no choice but to give her what she wants."

"If it gets Fallon and my brother back, then she can take what she wants from me. I don't care."

My team surrounds me. "If you're going rogue, so are we." Thorn stands tall, leading them.

"If we do this, there is no coming back. We'll all be out of a job that we love, and we may not all make it back alive."

"I'm in," Theo says.

"Me too." Fiona is at his side.

"Count me in," Mad Dog says.

"We'll find her," Tate and Honor say in unison.

"If you all are going, so am I," Lawson pipes in.

"Well, hell, I guess I'm in too." Remington throws his hat in the air.

"I'm new, but if your men are this loyal, you can count on me," Williams adds.

"I think you have your answer." Thorn slaps my shoulder. "If you're going after her, we're all going one way or another."

"Then pack up your gear. We're headed for battle." I get in my car and phone Commander Lukas.

"I quit, sir, and so do my men."

"Wait just a minute. What happened?"

"Fallon and Sean are gone. Nina forced their hands with some threat, and then she called me to gloat about it. I'm going after her along with my men."

He sighs. "Let me help you then. I'll get another team to cover the mission. The Gunners can handle Nina. I'll make it all look legit."

"I can't promise to go by the rules on this one, sir."

"I understand. I'll give you whatever resources I can. Off the books," he adds. "I want you to get this woman once and for all. Leave her body wherever she falls. I'll send in a team to clean up the mess."

"I don't know where we'll find her, but I may need backup wherever it is."

"I'll take care of it. In the meantime, I'll work on getting fake ID's for your men. You don't want her to be able to track your movement."

"I appreciate it, sir. Thanks."

"You're welcome, but I don't want to see your face again until she's been permanently taken out, no matter how long it takes."

"You have my word."

EPILOGUE

FALLON

"I can't believe she'll be two years old in a week." I stretch out in a chair and watch my daughter play in the sand.

"She looks so much like Derrick," Sean says as he helps her build a castle with a moat around it.

He's learned to read lips as well as sign. He's even taught his niece sign language. She picked it up so easily.

"She's just like him. Personality and all." Sadness fills my voice. "He'd love her so much."

"I'm sorry. I wish the two of you could've had a life together."

"Me too."

"Did I ever tell you I'm glad you brought me with you?"

"Multiple times." I laugh. I shade my eyes from the sun and look out over the water. "Do you think they're still out there looking for us?"

"I have no doubt that my brother has never quit looking for you."

"I don't know how it all played out. Maybe he thinks I left him at the altar."

"I'm sure Nina wanted her credit."

"Hopefully, she's gone by now, or she got bored with keeping track of us, and we could go home." It's wishful thinking on my part.

"You know that's not true. She leaves us clues that she knows where we are."

"It's been a few months since the last one. She's never gone that long before."

"If another month goes by and we've not received anything, we'll talk about it then. We've done everything we can do to keep them safe. We can't risk it if she's still watching us."

He's right, and I know it. I can't count how many times I've picked up the phone to call Rebel, only to hang up in tears. Especially when I found out I was pregnant. I wanted him to know so badly that he was going to be a father. I want Lily to know him. She deserves to have a father. I know Sean has played the role, but he's not Rebel.

When she was born, Nina sent gifts. She sneaked in the hospital nursery and took a picture of her. She made sure I knew about it when she called me. She was actually nice, for Nina. She's sent me several letters since then, telling me she's sorry that she took my life away but not sorry enough to set me free from our agreement. She sends Lily books with little notes in them. I always write her back to the only address she's ever given me, which is a post office box number.

It's taken me a while to find out who I am again. I got lost in all the mess with Nina. I'm still me, only stronger, braver, and self-confident. I've had to be for my daughter. I've kept up my self-defense classes, and I've stockpiled some weapons. I'm preparing for the day that Nina comes after us. I don't want to kill my sister, but I will never let her near Lily or Sean.

"I promise you one day, Lily, you will know your father," I say under my breath. For now, I'll watch and wait and cherish the moments I have with her, knowing I've kept her and Sean safe from my sister.

. . .

Living in the shadows. Risking everything for the man she loves. A dangerous game can only be won by becoming ruthless.

Click to continue to Fallon's Revenge.

ALSO BY KELLY MOORE

Whiskey River Road Series - Available on Audible

Coming Home, Book 1

Stolen Hearts, Book 2

Three Words, Book 3

Kentucky Rain, Book 4

Wild Ride, Book 5

Magnolia Mill, Book 6

Rough Road, Book 7

Lucky Man, Book 8 Aug 12 2021 (PreOrder)

The Broken Pieces Series in order

Broken Pieces

Pieced Together

Piece by Piece

Pieces of Gray

Syn's Broken Journey

Broken Pieces Box set Books 1-3

August Series in Order

Next August

This August

Seeing Sam

The Hitman Series- Previously Taking Down Brooklyn/The DC Seres

Stand By Me - On Audible as Deadly Cures

Stay With Me On Audible as Dangerous Captive

Hold Onto Me

Epic Love Stories Series can be read in any order

Say You Won't Let Go. Audiobook version

Fading Into Nothing Audiobook version

Life Goes On. Audiobook version

Gypsy Audiobook version

Jameson Wilde Audiobook version

Rescue Missions Series can be read in any order

Imperfect. On Audible

Blind Revenge

Fated Lives Series

Rebel's Retribution Books 1-4. Audible

Theo's Retaliation Books 5-7. Audible

Thorn's Redemption Audible

Fallon's Revenge Book 11 Audible

The Crazy Rich Davenports Season One in order of reading

The Davenports On Audible

Lucy

Yaya

Ford

Gemma

Daisy

The Wedding

Halloween Party

Bang Bang

Coffee Tea or Me

ABOUT THE AUTHOR

"This author has the magical ability to take an already strong and interesting plot and add so many unexpected twists and turns that it turns her books into a complete addiction for the reader." Dandelion Inspired Blog

Armed with books in the crook of my elbow, I can go anywhere. That's my philosophy! Better yet, I'll write the books that will take me on an adventure.

My heroes are a bit broken but will make you swoon. My heroines are their own kick-ass characters armed with humor and a plethora of sarcasm.

If I'm not tucked away in my writing den, with coffee firmly gripped in hand, you can find me with a book propped on my pillow, a pit bull lying across my legs, a Lab on the floor next to me, and two kittens running amuck.

My current adventure has me living in Idaho with my own gray-bearded hero, who's put up with my shenanigans for over thirty years, and he doesn't mind all my book boyfriends.

If you love romance, suspense, military men, lots of action and adventure infused with emotion, tear-worthy moments, and laugh-out-loud humor, dive into my books and let the world fall away at your feet.

WHISKEY RIVER ROAD

COMING HOME BOOK 1 SNEEK PEEK CHAPTER 1 CLEM CALHOUN

I park the truck on the edge of the concrete slab that has two other pickup trucks on it. Slowly getting out, I blow out a lengthy breath while trying to convince myself that I've done the right thing by coming home. I smooth down my long, chestnut-colored hair and adjust my simple army-green dress. Ethan gets out and walks around to my side of the truck.

"Are you ready?" He holds out his hand, and I take it. We head to the steps of the house, and he stops dead in his tracks.

"Why is there a shotgun leaning on the wall by the door?"

"That's not a shotgun. It's a rifle. I don't know, maybe they had some coyotes out here last night."

"Coyotes?" His gaze skims the area around the house.

The front door thunders open and my daddy, Chet Calhoun, steps out onto the painted wooden porch. "What the hell are you doing back here?" His heavy voice blares as his Adam's apple bobs. His silver hair and mustache haven't changed, but I don't recall the deep-seated wrinkles that now hang at his gray eyes. He's older but stands just as tall and brooding as he always has.

"I wanted to come home." I shrug one shoulder, unable to come up with anything else to say.

"You're not welcome here." He reaches behind him and grabs the rifle.

"Oh, Daddy, you're not going to shoot me." I brush the rifle downward, and he raises it again. "Then how about him." He waves it in Ethan's direction, and he scoots behind me.

Eighteen hours earlier...

"Does your family even know we're coming?" The springs creak in the seat as Ethan climbs in the passenger side of my old pickup truck. The knobs rattle as he shuts the door and he immediately tries to roll down the window but struggles with the broken crank.

"No, and trust me, it's better this way." I turn the key over, and nothing happens. With a slap of my hand on the cracked dash, the engine sputters as it comes to life. My lucky charm always works. Its old bones make all kinds of noises, including a backfire that has Ethan jumping in his seat and banging his head on the bare ceiling of the truck.

"What the hell, Clem? Why do you still have this old truck anyway? Even the bumper doesn't look like it wants to hang around on it. It's holding on by one bolt. It's a piece of shit. Is it even going to get us to Kentucky?" He rubs the side of his head.

"Ahhh, cover your ears, Lizzy." I gasp and pat the dash like I'm consoling her. "She and I have been through a lot together. I'm pretty sure she'll outlive me. Besides, once we get to the ranch, she'll fit right in." The sound of the gears shifting into drive drops heavily into place with a sharp grind. The engine gives one last hiccup before it jerks into motion. I glance over at Ethan, and he's already digging through the bag of junk food and drinks that he bought when I stopped to fill up the gas tank.

It's early, and the heat is radiating off the

sunbaked long, narrow highway. The glass in my window makes a rubbing noise as I exert pressure to turn the window crank. It stops at halfway and won't go any further, but it's enough to let a breeze flow through once I open the sliding back window. The wind sends my dog tags hanging from the rearview mirror into a tornado spin.

Over the sound of the wind whipping through, I hear Ethan slurping his drink through a straw. I cut my gaze to him, and he shrugs.

He starts feeling around the seats and the center console. "Where are the cup holders?"

"You'll have to hold it between your thighs because there isn't any."

"Jesus, Clem. Why couldn't we have driven my new car?"

"Because that thing is pretty and a Corvette has no place where we're going?"

"You make it sound like we're going to *The Hills Have Eyes*."

I giggle at his reference to the scary movie. "Have you ever been to the hills of Kentucky?" I add, in my not so frightening southern drawl.

"No. You know I'm a city boy from New York, but you're scaring me just a little." He pinches his fingers together.

"How did you and I ever become best friends?" I can't help but laugh at him.

He finally gets his window rolled down and hangs his arm out. "I helped you get through basic training, and then you wouldn't quit following me around." His smile goes from ear to ear.

He's right. I didn't know a soul and was terrified once I enlisted. I had no idea why this charming city boy helped me, but he did. I could've easily fallen for his good looks and lean body. He has that all-American boy thing going on that all the women love. Jet-black hair, perfect teeth, and smile. Bright blue eyes that could make any normal girl's libido rage.

I was still reeling from walking out on Boone on our wedding day. I haven't spoken a word to him since. I wasn't ready to jump into another relationship, much less a fuck fest with a hot soldier boy. I wanted to find out who I was besides a girl that was raised to be prim and proper but born with a dirty mind. After having my mouth washed out with soap enough, I learned to keep my thoughts to myself.

"It was you who kept pursuing me." I snort.

He reaches over and spins the volume on the radio. He immediately starts humming to the country song playing. I introduced him to it, and now he's a die-hard fan. I tap the steering wheel to the beat of the music and enjoy listening to him.

It isn't long before I glance over and see his head lying against the doorframe with drool coming out of the corner of his mouth. Not a sexy look on him. It will be a boring eighteen-hour drive from Fort Carson to Salt Lick, Kentucky if he's going to sleep half the ride.

I pull my dark, round sunglasses from the visor and focus on the drive. I can't help but wonder how my family will take me coming back. I was just a young girl when I left. Returning at twenty-eight, I have a better perspective on what I want out of life, and the things I once hated about the ranch, I now think fondly of and have an aching in my heart to return. My older sister Ellie and I have written for years, and she's kept me somewhat in the know about Mom, Daddy, and our two brothers. The last email I got from her was pretty nonspecific. She said there was trouble at the ranch, and Daddy's health wasn't the best. I figured now was the best time to return. I'm free of the army and can start a new life. But first I need to make some amends.

Daddy and I used to be close, but I'm sure Boone's heart wasn't the only one broken that day. I love my father, but he was always so controlling of his family. *"We're cattle ranchers and racehorse breeders and trainers. That's what we do, and that's what each of you will do."* I can still hear his firm voice in my head. He was the one that insisted that I marry Boone. He'd hired him as the lead trainer when I was sixteen years old. My love for the horses had me following in his shadow like a little lost puppy dog. It didn't help that I was a horny teenage girl, and all I could think about was what was under the fly of his faded blue jeans. He was five years older than me. He only thought of me as the boss's baby daughter until I turned twenty. I was a late bloomer, and my girls didn't blossom until then. That's when he started to look at me like a man looks at a woman, and I ate it up.

He taught me everything I know about training racehorses and other things. I was comfortable with him and enjoyed his company. There was a raw sexual force between us that I didn't understand. My father saw that. Well, not the sexual part. He would've skinned my hide. He pushed us together. He said we'd make a powerful team in the industry.

Boone was sweet in a rugged sort of way. He'd flex his biceps, and my sex drive would approach a meltdown level. I was in a constant state of a puddled mess between my legs just looking at him.

He was a true cowboy from Texas. The song, "Save a Horse (Ride a Cowboy)," always skirted around my mind when I was near him.

My dad found him hanging around the tracks and took him under his wing. His dark-brown sexy, soft curls and killer smile made it easy to fall for him. I loved him, but I wanted more out of life, and he deserved someone that didn't feel stuck. In hindsight, I picked a really bad day to decide I couldn't be who he or my father wanted me to be.

Seven years in the army, I grew up. I traveled overseas and learned the cybersecurity industry. I only ended up in Colorado six months ago. It was the first time I'd been in the same place as Ethan since we were assigned to an army base in Europe. I stayed there, and he went on to Germany. By then, I only saw him as a friend and not someone I wanted to hop in the sack with.

I know I should've made more attempts to talk to my family after I left, but Daddy was so angry. He told Ellie to tell me to never come home again. He wouldn't take any calls from me, and he forbid my mom to talk to me. My older brother Wyatt is thick as thieves with my father. He lives and breathes the business, so he only does what he's told to do.

My brother Bear, who's only a year older than

me, was too busy being a ladies' man to care what was going on with anyone's life but his own. Ellie's always been a sweet, innocent girl and loved the ranch. She swore she'd never leave.

I've been lost in my thoughts for hours, listening to Ethan snore. I reach over and shake his leg. "Hey, I need to stop for fuel and to use the ladies' room."

He wipes the drool off his face with the back of his hand. "How long have I been sleeping?"

"Four hours. You never even woke up the last time I fueled up." I pull off the highway into a mom-and-pop station. Ethan helps out by pumping the fuel while I run inside.

When we get back onto the road, Ethan is driving. He keeps trying to adjust the seat to fit his lengthy legs. "You really haven't spoken to Boone since you left him at the altar?"

"No. Ellie said he didn't want anything to do with me. I can't blame him."

"You've remained pretty closed-lipped about the story other than the basics, even from me. Why don't you tell me the details, being that I'm going to meet all of them? I think you should spill it."

Resting my head on the back of the seat, I let the wind cool my face and bring back clear memories. "I remember Ellie zipping me up and watching me in the mirror. I'd been in my own head, frantic about what I was about to do. The dress suddenly felt like hot glue on my skin. My head started spinning, and I felt woozy. Pictures of my future flashed before my eyes. I recall telling my sister, 'I...I can't do this.' I ripped the veil and the flowers out of my hair that she had spent the last hour fixing.

"She asked what I was talking about. She kept telling me that Boone and half the town was waiting for me in the church.

"My chair scooted across the floor as I fought to stand because my legs felt like wet noodles trying to hold myself up. My dress got caught underneath one the legs, and it ripped a layer of frill off. I screamed for her to unzip me. I twisted my arm over my head to tug at the zipper, but my hand was shaking so much I couldn't get a grip on it."

I stuff my hands between my legs and look down. "Ellie kept saying she didn't understand. I can still feel her pulling the zipper all the way to my lower back, and I shrugged out of my dress.

"I told her that I did love Boone, but that I was only twenty-one years old. I wanted more out of life than the ranch and racehorses. If I had married him, it would be all I'd ever know. Traveling from horse track to horse track would be all I'd see of the world.

I needed more, I wanted more, and it was such a confusing time for me.

"She cried, telling me that I'd been born and bred into this. That Daddy told her I'd become one of the best horse trainers he'd ever seen.

"I couldn't get in my skinny jeans fast enough. I remember telling her, that's what he wants for my life, and what about what I want? That never mattered to him. She tried to convince me that it did, but I knew better. Then she kept repeating the question, what about Boone?

"I told her that was just it. I didn't know what I wanted, but I needed to figure it out before I settled down into a life I would regret."

I look back up to see Ethan watching me from the corner of his eye. "I finished dressing as she kept trying to convince me to stay. She knew I'd spoken to a recruiter and had been talking about it for days. I tugged my cowgirl boots on and worked on pulling the hundreds of bobby pins out of my hair. She couldn't believe I was really walking out. A runaway bride. I grabbed the suitcase that I had packed for my honeymoon to nowhere and my purse. I asked her to help me. When she didn't answer, I told her I was leaving one way or another and marched to the back door of the church. I was terrified when I peeked out the door to make sure no one would see me. I ran to Lizzy that was parked underneath the shade of some trees.

"I was so afraid I'd get caught because Ellie was running behind me screaming my name ,begging me not to leave. I yanked the Chevy door open, and the last thing I said to her was to tell Boone I was sorry. When I drove off, I saw her in my rearview mirror, waving frantically and tears streaming down her face. When I got to the end of the dirt road, I hesitated only for a second. I clearly remember whispering the words, goodbye dirt road. I never slowed down again."

He's quiet for a moment as if he's mulling around what I've told him. "Does Boone still work for your dad?"

"Yeah. I've been reading in the racehorse magazines that the horse he's been training for the past three years is winning at all the tracks. Sounds like he's got a good chance at the Kentucky Derby this year."

"Wow. Has your dad ever had a winning horse before?"

"Back in 2009, he had a horse that won. The racehorse he has now, Whiskey River, is from the same bloodline."

"Where do they come up with horse names. I mean, some of them sound like royalty." The truck bounces over a pothole.

I grab onto to the rough dash. "Some of them are considered royalty and treated as such."

"I'm looking forward to seeing what your life was like growing up on a ranch."

"I didn't appreciate it enough."

"Do you regret leaving?"

"I don't regret going into the army and all the experiences I've had. What I do regret is leaving the way I did. I hurt my family and Boone. If they'll let me, I want to make it up to them, but my dad isn't the most forgiving person in the world. He's perfected holding a grudge to high levels."

"And what about the man you left at the altar? Do you want to make things up to him too?"

"There's no way I ever can. He's moved on with his life and so have I."

* * *

We stopped at a small hotel for the night and ate at a rowdy steak house. We got up early, bought our coffee, and hit the road.

With two more hours to go, we start getting into

farmland. Broken wooden fences on one side of the narrow road, barbed wire on the other. Clumps of dandelions and foxtail border the bluegrass fields between the road and the fencing. Harvested round hay bales are sitting in a crop stubble. Cows graze near an old rotting barn structure forgotten in a field. The sky always seems bluer here and filled with birds flying overhead. A hawk is perched on a wooden fence post, waiting to find a field mouse for its supper.

We pass a farmer wearing overalls, who's pushing a wheel barrel and chewing on a stalk of sweet grass. Off in the distance, there's a tractor throwing up a plume of dust in its wake.

"Are you getting nervous?" Ethan has his arm out the window, making waving motions with his hand.

"A little, but I'm bound and determined not to let Daddy keep me away from my family any longer."

"Good for you. I'll be by your side unless he has a shotgun, then you're on your own." He laughs.

"Oh, my father has a multitude of guns."

His eyes get round as saucers. "He's not going to shoot you is he?"

"I don't think he'll go to that extreme, but you might want to wear a bulletproof vest," I tease him.

"Ha-ha, not funny."

Gravel crackles under my tires as I turn onto a long, winding drive and stop by the green street sign.

"Whiskey River Road," Ethan reads and then shoulders the door open to get out. "That's where the horse's name came from."

I step onto the gravel and drag my sunglasses to the top of my nose and look down the road that leads to my family. The fragrance of the lavender flocks smells like home, and I can taste the pollen filtering through the dry air. The road turns to red clay dirt about a quarter mile down. I recognize the familiar tracks in the gravel from a horse trailer being hauled by an oversized truck.

Ethan's army boots scuff in the rocks. "Take my picture under the street sign." He points to it and smiles.

I take my phone out of the side panel in the door of the truck and snap his picture.

"You're almost home." He climbs back in the passenger seat.

I put Lizzy in gear and slowly head down the uneven road. Ethan fiddles with the radio and stops when he hears the song "Sweet Home Alabama."

"Wrong state, but it'll still work." He turns up the volume.

I laugh and join him in singing it. The potholes

along the dirt road jar my teeth and seriously mess with my rendition of the song, but I refuse to let it ruin the moment. I need to keep the good mood I'm in to be able to face my family, more specifically, Daddy.

Made in the USA
Middletown, DE
30 August 2022